stardust stables

A STAR IS BORN

stardust stables

A STAR IS BORN

SABLE HAMILTON

Stripes

STRIPES PUBLISHING
An imprint of Little Tiger Press
1 The Coda Centre, 189 Munster Road,
London SW6 6AW

A paperback original
First published in Great Britain in 2013

ISBN: 978-1-84715-235-0

A CIP catalogue record for this book is
available from the British Library.

Printed and bound in the UK.

2 4 6 8 10 9 7 5 3 1

For Shelley, my fearless friend

chapter one

"Hey, Kami, and welcome!" Jack Jones, owner of Stardust stunt-riding stables, stretched out a hand.

Kami Cooper grinned back at him. "Hey," she murmured. She and her dad had made the two-hour drive from their home at Elk Creek. They'd dropped off her bags in the girls' living quarters, and then she'd waved her dad goodbye. Now, day one at the Colorado stables had kicked into action. Boy was she excited.

"Good timing," Jack told her. He was tall and lean, around forty years old and his face was creased into a broad, welcoming smile. "Lizzie's working some of our horses and riders in the round pen. Come take a look."

She followed him across the corral, past a low red barn and a row of wooden stalls towards a fenced arena.

"Hey, guys," Kami murmured to each of the ponies looking out over the stall doors - a pretty palomino, a high-class, bored-looking sorrel, a cute brown-and-white Paint and a beautiful light grey Quarter Horse with a long black mane.

As the ponies snickered at the newcomer, a boy at work in one of the empty stalls popped up his head. He was around fourteen, tall and slim, and wearing a pale blue T-shirt and a baseball cap with the peak reversed to protect the back of his neck from the fierce sun.

"Hey, Tom, meet Kami Cooper. Her folks run Elk Creek Guest Ranch a couple of hours south-west of here. She's joined us for the summer, so you'll be seeing plenty of her."

Tom nodded, then gave Kami a quick smile.

"Tom's a regular member of our team," Jack explained. "This is his second season here, along with his sister, Kellie. They live thirty minutes away, just outside Colorado Springs, so they get to work here at Christmas and weekends, too."

"So, how did Jack and Lizzie find you?" Tom came out of the stall, brushing straw from his jeans, and followed Jack and Kami to the round pen.

"I entered a contest in Clearwater County," Kami replied, looking away shyly. Tom's direct gaze and lazy drawl made her feel even more self-conscious than when she first shook hands with Jack. She blushed and swept her light blonde hair forward to hide her face.

"Lizzie was in the area scouting for talent," Jack explained. "The Clearwater show attracts some terrific junior riders. Lizzie saw Kami win the barrel-racing contest by a mile and thought she'd be a great addition to the team."

"Awesome! Which horse will she be riding?" Tom asked.

Jack shrugged. "I have no idea – that's Lizzie's deal."

"Just so long as it's not Legend," Tom joked. "I'll kill anyone who tries to take my palomino away from me!" He came up to Kami as they reached the arena fence, his grey eyes twinkling. "So you reckon you can make it as a stunt rider?"

"I don't know about that," Kami answered tentatively. This was all so new – the sunny corral that nestled at the foot of the mountains, the big old barn to one side and ranch house to the other, with the round pen on the near side of a fast-running creek. Beyond the creek there was a green meadow where horses grazed. And now there was this gangly boy with a cheeky smile and cute sticky-out ears asking questions and grinning at her.

"Sure you can – you're the best young rider in your home county," Jack said to her. "Your dad told Lizzie they put you in the saddle at the age of two."

"But I don't know any stunts." Kami gasped as the three riders in the round pen galloped their mounts round the pen under Lizzie's instruction. "Not yet anyway." They came so close she could almost reach over the fence to touch them. She caught the smell of sweat and dust, felt the dirt kicked up by the horses' hooves sting her cheeks.

"Hey!" A girl in a pink shirt on a sorrel mare waved as she galloped by, seemingly super-glued to the saddle. Her glossy, long dark hair hung loose beneath her safety helmet and she wore shades to protect her eyes from the sun. Horse and rider in perfect harmony – it was beautiful.

"That's Alisa on Diabolo," Jack told Kami. "She's a pro. Watch and learn!"

"Hi there!" A second girl greeted Kami from the back of a dark bay Quarter Horse. Dressed in a yellow plaid shirt beneath her blue body armour, she rode her pony bareback.

"Kellie and Dylan." Tom took over the introductions. "Kellie's my kid sister. She's thirteen."

"The same age as me." Kami watched with awe as Kellie suddenly switched from sitting to crouching on Dylan's hindquarters. Then she went from crouching to standing with arms spread wide.

"Lizzie's teaching them a new trick," said Tom.

Kellie and Dylan caught up with Alisa and Diabolo, then Kellie leaned sideways and shifted her weight across so that she stood astride the two ponies.

"Roman riding," Jack explained, watching Kami's amazed reaction. "Kellie's a natural stunt rider. Now take a look at Hayley on Cool Kid."

Kami switched her attention to the third horse and rider – a stocky little Paint ridden by a skinny girl with a long dark braid that made her look younger than the others. Her pony kicked up a cloud of dirt as she slid him to a stop. She sprang from the saddle and gave Cool Kid a tap on his hindquarters. The pony set off again at a trot. Hayley chased after him, came alongside, then vaulted back into the saddle.

"Think you can do that?" Tom asked with a grin.

Kami frowned and shook her head. These girls were seriously good. Now Lizzie called in other riders - a couple more girls and some boys, until there was a total of ten riders working their horses in the pen.

"You will, no problem," Jack told her kindly. "Everyone feels a little nervous at first. But you just have to put in the hours. Stunt riding is one part talent and three parts hard work."

Kami nodded as she watched riders fling themselves sideways, then hang from their saddles by their legs ("A drag," Tom explained), riders clinging to the saddle horn and throwing their weight forward towards their pony's head ("A front wing") - exciting, dangerous stunts that she was afraid she'd never learn.

"Lizzie, do you have time to introduce Kami to her pony?" Jack called out as his wife walked by.

"Hey, Kami!" Lizzie had been focused on teaching and hadn't noticed the new arrival. Now she came out of the round pen to greet her. "How was your journey? Did you drop off your stuff in the girls' quarters? You're rooming with Alisa - I'm sure she'll show you around. How about getting something to eat?"

"No, I'm good, thanks." Kami was glad to say hi to a familiar face at last. She recognized Lizzie from Clearwater – she was not tall, but very slim, with blonde hair tied back under a black Stetson and gold hoop earrings that added a touch of glamour to her western outfit of dark shirt, blue jeans and heeled boots.

"So, you're keen to meet the horse you'll be working with?" asked Lizzie, picking up immediately on Kami's anxiety.

"Yes, please."

Lizzie beckoned for Kami to follow and led the way across the corral towards the barn.

"Don't be nervous," she said, turning to Kami with a smile. "His name's Magic. You're going to love him."

"I'm never, never going to be that good!" Kami confided her fears to Magic after Lizzie had gone to the office to order more grain for the horses, leaving her alone with her new horse in his straw-lined stall.

Magic nudged her gently with his nose. He was the pale dappled grey with the long dark mane who she'd noticed in the stalls earlier that morning.

Now, close up, she saw that he had the biggest, gentlest brown eyes, the softest muzzle and the longest, thickest, glossiest mane. Lizzie had been right – for Kami it was love at first sight.

"You know it was tough leaving my pony, Columbine, behind," she said sadly. "She's back home in Elk Creek. I love her, too, of course. She's a gorgeous sorrel and I've known her since I was eight. But no way could I bring Columbine to Stardust because she's a working ranch horse and my folks need her. I won't see her again until I leave here in the fall. I'm sure going to miss her."

Magic gave her another nudge.

"OK, so I'm a decent rider," Kami confessed to him in a soft voice, trying to be positive. "But no way am I as good as Alisa, Kellie and Hayley. I'm no superstar."

The beautiful grey Quarter Horse rustled his feet in the straw.

Kami put her arms round his neck in the quiet warmth of his stall and sighed. "I just hope you're not going to be disappointed in me."

Magic turned his head and nuzzled her cheek. His soft nose tickled and she smiled. "Yeah, I hear you," she murmured. "You're telling me not to worry – you and me, we're a perfect fit!"

"So, Kami, how do you like your horse?" Alisa asked.

It was just after lunch and she, Hayley and Kellie had split off from the boys and invited Kami to join them at the cold drinks machine behind the tack room. They took cans of Coke, paper cups and ice from the machine, then sat together round a rough wooden table, under the shade of a big yellow sun umbrella.

"I love him," Kami sighed. The drink was cool and fizzy and she needed it after two hours scooping up horse manure in the baking hot corral with Tom and two other boys named Zak and Ross.

"I can't believe my brother had you scooping poop," Kellie remarked. The hatband of her safety helmet had left a red mark round her forehead. Like Tom, she had clear grey eyes. "That's the worst job in the world!"

"Nope, that would be walking out to the meadow at five in the morning to bring in the horses," Alisa disagreed. "I'm talking December – it's still dark and the temperature's ten degrees below zero."

"Yet still she looks like she just stepped out of a Wrangler ad – not a hair out of place," Hayley joked.

"I do not," Alisa protested, but Kami believed Hayley. She'd already decided that her new roommate was just about the most elegant girl she'd ever met.

"And, Kami, I bet you thought stunt riding was all glamour and glitz," Hayley laughed. "They didn't tell you about the poop."

"It's OK, I live on a guest ranch." The three girls seemed super-friendly and Kami started to relax. "I'm used to it."

"We already know." Kellie had a round face and a big smile. "We also know you picked up first prize in the barrel racing at the Clearwater show. You've been competing forever, since you were five, which is eight years back. We heard your story from my brother Tom."

"Lizzie is a great scout," Alisa assured Kami. "She knows talent when she sees it. Jack's the one who has the contacts in the movies and TV. Once upon a time he was an actor and stunt rider himself, so he knows directors and other actors in the business, plus the agents who find most of our work and sort out the contracts. He deals with the money side of things."

"Lizzie and Jack work together on choreographing the stunts," Kellie explained. "They're both top names in the industry."

"Enough. I bet Kami already knows the history of Stardust!" Hayley cried, throwing her empty Coke can into the bin.

"No, I want to hear this." Kami took another swig from her cup and settled down to listen to her new friends. This was going to be a great experience, she decided – learning amazing stunts and chilling with the girls.

Kellie took over the story from Alisa. "Lizzie Jones is only the best horse trainer this side of the Rockies and she's into natural horsemanship methods, which means listening to what the horse is telling you and never using any force."

"Which makes us totally respect her," Alisa added. "She married Jack three years back, just before he joined Stardust Stables. Now they're in competition with Lizzie's ex – a guy named Pete Mason. He's set up a rival stunt-riding stables named High Noon."

"Yawn yawn," Hayley objected. "Come on, guys – there are horses to ride."

"No, Kami should know the basic insider facts." Alisa ignored Hayley, who shrugged her shoulders, then went to the corral to saddle up. "It's not been easy for them to keep the business going, especially since Pete often plays dirty by deliberately bad-mouthing Stardust and undercutting the fees we charge. In my book that amounts to stealing work that should rightly come to us."

"So what Alisa is trying to say is that we never know for sure when the next big deal is coming along," Kellie explained. "But, hey, until it does we just train and train until our butts are sore!"

"Talking of which," Alisa got up from the table, "I have to slap a saddle on Diabolo and take him down to the creek. This afternoon Jack wants to rehearse the 'fall from the horse and land in water' trick."

"After that he's teaching Dylan to ride through fire," Kellie added. "You think I'm kidding, Kami, but I'm not!"

"Never!" Kami promised Magic as she led him into the corral, tethered him to the rail and started to saddle him up for her first session in the round pen. "Never and no way will I ever take you near flames!" Horses hated fire – it was their worst nightmare.

"She talks to her horse!"

Kami swung round, blushing furiously. Tom was right behind her, leading his horse, Legend, into the corral.

"She talks to her horse and expects him to answer," Tom teased. "Actually, it's kind of cute."

Kami felt hotter and more embarrassed than ever. "Anyway, I *won't* take Magic near fire!" she declared. "I'd never do anything that would put my horse in danger."

Tom only looked at her and grinned. Then he turned to his horse. "You hear that, Legend? No fire stunts for Kami and Magic."

Legend, the palomino, tossed her blonde mane.

"Legend says not to worry – there's always a rep from the American Humane Association on set, so 'No horse gets injured in the making of these films'."

There was something about Tom that made Kami smile. "I'm late. I have to meet Lizzie in the round pen." She untied Magic's lead rope and walked him out of the corral, feeling her stomach begin to knot up. What if it turned out she was no good at stunt riding?

How could she bear to go home and admit to her mom and dad that she wasn't going to perform any daredevil tricks in front of the camera after all?

"Hey, Kami." Lizzie Jones was already there, smiling down from her beautiful sorrel mare. "This is Sugar. And don't worry – we won't try anything too tricky this afternoon."

Kami swallowed hard. She felt Magic walking calmly at her side and this gave her confidence as she fastened her helmet, then swung herself into the saddle. "Good boy," she breathed, and she squeezed her legs against his sides.

First task – trotting round the arena, with Lizzie watching the movement of every muscle in horse and rider.

Second – squeezing again and sitting low in the saddle. Then, with a click of the tongue, easing Magic into a lope round the rim of the round pen.

By now Tom had finished grooming Legend in the corral and he and Zak had come to the fence to watch.

"Don't you have work to do?" Lizzie called when she spotted them.

"Nope," they insisted. "We're chilling."

"Well just try not to draw attention to yourselves, however hard that might be." Lizzie grinned, then gave Kami her next instruction. "Lope Magic until he's totally relaxed."

Kami loved the smoothness of Magic's stride. She loved his intelligence and everything about him. The sun shone down, sending the temperature soaring. Kami couldn't help smiling. This was as close to heaven as she ever hoped to get.

"OK, the first stunt you're going to learn this afternoon is how to stand up in the saddle," Lizzie explained, as she and Sugar came alongside. "Watch – I'll show you."

Kami concentrated hard as Lizzie kicked her feet free of the stirrups and hunched her knees towards her chest, then let go of the reins. As Sugar loped on, Lizzie leaned forward and tucked her feet right under her. Then she raised herself into a standing position and kept her balance by spreading her arms wide. "See?"

Kami nodded. Her mouth was dry, her palms sweaty.

"Try the first part," Lizzie told her. "Kick free of your stirrups and let go of the reins."

Kami did it. Magic didn't miss a beat. His ears were

swivelled back in her direction, waiting for her next move.

"Now pull your knees towards your chest."

She did as Lizzie instructed. She was perched on the shiny saddle and her balance wasn't quite right. Magic loped on. Kami leaned into the bend.

"Lean out," Lizzie called. But it was too late.

Leaning into the curve, Kami lost control. Then, as she felt herself slipping, she tried to grab the saddle horn.

"Whoa!" Tom and Zak called as she hit the ground.

Kami lay there as Lizzie caught hold of Magic's rein and brought him to a halt.

"You OK?" Lizzie checked.

Kami nodded. The only thing that hurt was her pride. She stood up and dusted herself down, then took a deep breath. "Sorry," she mumbled. Forget the glamour of stunt riding – she realized this was going to be pure grind and sweat, plus cuts and bruises, and maybe even a cracked rib or two along the way.

"No problem," Lizzie said. "Are you ready to try again?"

"This time without eating dirt," Kami promised Magic. She rubbed her sore back.

"You're not the first and you won't be the last to fall off your horse when you're training to be a stunt rider," Lizzie grinned. "Come on, let's go again."

chapter two

Night was the loneliest time.

Kami had been fine all day - making new friends and bonding with Magic. But now as she lay in bed staring up at the sky as moonlight poured through the gap in the drapes, she missed her home so much that her heart ached.

She missed her mom and her dad. She missed her cat, Squeaky, purring and licking her face to wake her in the morning, and most of all she missed her own sorrel pony, her beloved Columbine.

The clock at her bedside ticked as she watched the clouds drift across the face of the moon. All was quiet in the girls' accommodation. Kami stared at the stars until at last her eyes closed and she drifted off to sleep.

The stars were shining and she was riding Columbine through the spring meadow at Elk Creek, feeling the wind in her hair, hearing the thud of hooves on soft turf. Next thing the sun was up and they loped through the creek, kicking up spray. Then they were way up in the mountains with no one else around, just chilling and taking in the view of Clearwater Lake far below. She saw Columbine's face in close-up – her wonderful dark eyes so gentle and trusting, the white flash running down her nose, the unruly, nut-brown mane that refused to fall neatly to one side.

"However hard I brush, I never can get that looking right," Kami sighed as she stepped up into the saddle and rode Columbine proudly into the arena at the county show.

The crowd cheered and she woke up with a start.

In the small, simple bedroom at Stardust she heard the sound of Alisa's quiet, even breathing. There was nothing here but two beds, each with a bedside table and a lamp, and across the room a shared closet. On the table next to Kami was a framed picture of herself and Columbine, proud winners of the barrel-racing contest. Lying in the dark, Kami felt tears come to her eyes.

"The first forty-eight hours are the worst," Kellie assured her over a breakfast of crispy bacon and hash browns.

All the kids at Stardust Stables - twelve in total - were up at dawn and assigned to various tasks before breakfast. Some brought horses in from the meadow, some dealt with extra grain for the horses who needed it, some shifted bales of hay while others scooped poop in the corral. Then they all took breakfast with Jack and Lizzie in the old ranch house before starting their training routines in the round pen.

At the start of Kami's second day, Kellie had made a beeline for Kami as soon as she arrived in the dining room. "You look like you need to talk."

"It's OK, I'm good," Kami insisted, even though her eyes pricked from lack of sleep and she pushed the bacon round her plate without eating it.

"No, you're not. You're homesick." Checking that Kami didn't want her hash browns, Kellie scooped the heap of fried potatoes on to her own plate. "We all are the first time we come here. This is my third year at Stardust, but I remember my first time like it was yesterday."

"Hey, Kellie, hey, Kami," Alisa and Hayley called from across the noisy room. They were sitting with a girl whom Kami hadn't met yet - small, with blonde hair like Kami's. She was staring curiously at the new arrival.

"That's Becca," Kellie told Kami. "She's a great rider..."

"...But?" Kami felt there was a "but" in there somewhere.

"No buts. Just know that Becca has been working with Lizzie forever. This is her sixth year. She's appeared in all the *River Eden* movies, plus the *Gold Rush* TV series - I could go on and on. So anyway, like I was saying, get through today and you'll begin to love it here, OK?"

"Thanks." Kami gave Kellie a grateful smile. "I didn't get the chance to ask you yesterday - how did you and Dylan get on with riding through fire?"

Kellie shrugged. "Dylan was spooked by the flames so we took it nice and slow. It turns out Jack thinks he may not be the best choice for scenes taking place in burning barns etcetera. Diabolo's better. Dylan's good with explosions, though, and no horse plays dead better than my own sweet boy."

"I've got so much to learn." Kami thought through all the stunts she couldn't yet perform and sighed.

Kellie grinned. "So, what are you waiting for?" She shovelled down the last of the hash browns and marched Kami out of the dining room. "Oh, and by the way, Tom really likes you," she added, arching her eyebrows and grinning broadly. "He's a typical boy so you'll never get him to admit it up front, but I'm his sister and I know these things!"

Still blushing, Kami walked Magic in from the meadow and tethered him to a rail in the corral, where she picked up a brush and began work to get the caked dirt out of his dappled coat. Becca's horse, Pepper, stood beside them. He was another grey, similar to Magic but bigger and with a white mane and tail.

"Let me see that brush," Becca said, coming out of the tack room.

Kami handed it over and waited.

"This belongs to me and Pepper," Becca informed her without any trace of a smile. "Everyone has their own grooming kit. You'll find yours in the tack room, on the shelf labelled 'Magic'."

D'oh! Kami felt two inches tall. She went inside and found Tom, Zak and Ross sweeping out the tack room. The boys left off talking the moment she arrived.

"Hey," Kami mumbled.

"Hey, Kami." It was Ross who answered, while Zak elbowed Tom in the ribs and sent him sprawling behind the rail of head collars.

Awkward! Remembering what Kellie had told her, she made a quick grab for Magic's brush and curry comb and headed back out into the corral.

Luckily Becca had already saddled Pepper and was heading towards the round pen, leaving Kami free to groom her pony until his dappled coat shone in the sunlight and his mane and tail were smooth and tangle-free. *Chill!* She told herself. *This is only your second day. You can't expect to know how things work around here.*

Magic tossed his head. Then he softly nuzzled her hand, as if to say, *Stick with me, kid. We'll be totally fine!*

Kami smiled and stroked his neck. She had his saddle on and was busy with his bridle when Tom stepped out on to the tack-room porch.

"Sorry, I don't want you to think we were talking about you back there," he mumbled shyly. Then his cheeky grin broke through. "Actually, we were, though. Zak and Ross were giving me a hard time."

"No problem," Kami grinned back. "I already had the same treatment from your sister."

"Jeez!"

"Yeah."

"Anyway, I thought I'd just say hi."

"Yeah, hi!" Blushing furiously, Kami stepped into the saddle and followed Becca and Pepper into the round pen.

"Good luck," Tom called after her. "You're going to do great – trust me!"

★★★★★

"At Stardust we work as a team," Lizzie reminded Kami and Becca. Today the owner of the stables was on foot, ready to work again with Kami on how to stand in the saddle. "Becca, you're going to ride Pepper alongside Kami and Magic, showing Kami exactly what to do. Kami, you're going to copy Becca move for move."

The girls nodded.

"Don't overthink this," Lizzie advised Kami. "Relax and be confident that you can do whatever I ask. And remember - keep your eye on Becca. She, along with Alisa, is the most experienced junior stunt rider we have."

Another nod from Kami and they were ready to go, side by side, from walk into trot and then into canter, perfectly in time as Lizzie stood in the centre of the round pen and called out instructions.

"Kick free of the stirrups, drop your reins."

The horses loped on as both girls did as Lizzie said.

"Pull your knees towards your chest."

Kami copied Becca, this time making sure that she didn't shift her weight as Pepper and Magic kept pace round the outside of the pen.

"Now stand!" Lizzie called.

Kami glanced sideways to see Becca make one smooth movement from sitting to standing. She held her breath and copied.

Wow! This time she was actually keeping her balance and standing on the saddle. Magic was loping on.

"Good!" Lizzie called. "OK, now sit."

Kami had to look hard to see what Becca did. It involved keeping your back straight and bending your knees, then sliding back down into the saddle - smoothly.

Ouch!

"Not so good!" Lizzie groaned as Kami thudded down into the saddle. "But you get the general idea."

Giving a sideways glance, Kami thought she saw a smug grin flit across Becca's face. Then again, she could have imagined it.

"Do it again," Lizzie urged. "And this time, Kami, let's make that transition from standing to sitting a little smoother, for the sake of your poor butt, if nothing else!"

"We really need to secure that *Moonlight Dream* contract before Pete steps in and grabs it from under our noses."

Kami was three days into her training when she overheard a conversation between Jack and Lizzie at breakfast on Thursday morning. It was her first morning off and she'd slept in. The dining room was almost empty. She glanced round, wondering where Alisa and the rest had gone.

"I've been looking at our spreadsheets," Lizzie said to Jack. "Our profits are way down compared with this time last year."

Jack thought for a while. "Matt Harrison is working on the *Moonlight* movie. I worked with him ten years back. You want me to call him?"

"Do you think he can help?"

Jack shrugged. "Maybe he could put Stardust's name into the hat instead of leaving everything in the hands of our agent, the way we usually do."

"It's worth a try," Lizzie agreed. "But Matt's only an actor in the movie – it's not his decision."

"Sure, it's down to the director, Brad Morley. And I know for a fact he's been having a hard time finding the right stunt double for Coreen."

"OK, so call Matt." Lizzie looked up to see Kami hovering uncertainly with her plate of eggs and wheat toast. "Come and sit," she invited, making room for her at the table. "We won't talk business – I promise!"

Jack smiled. "I hear you're making good progress, Kami."

"Yeah – tell Jack what you've learned in three short

days," Lizzie urged.

Kami counted the stunts on her fingers. "Standing in the saddle - check. Roman riding - check, front wing - check. And I have the cuts and bruises to prove it," she laughed.

"I'm impressed." Jack grinned. "No regrets?"

Kami shook her head. "I still have a lot to learn, but I'm definitely having fun and I'm making some great new friends."

"You like the horse we chose for you?"

"Magic is perfect," Kami grinned.

"How's the homesickness?"

"Not too bad, thanks. I miss my horse back home, though." *And my cat, and my mom...*

"The good news is, she'll still be there waiting for you in the fall." Jack obviously understood and tried to make Kami feel better. "Until then, we'll do our best to keep you busy. Who knows, if you work hard enough, there could be a part for you in this major movie we were discussing."

"But no pressure," Lizzie broke in with a laugh. "Especially not today. Why not just chill? Some of the girls have already packed a sack lunch and ridden out."

"Really?" Kami hadn't realized quite how long she'd

stayed in bed.

"Alisa said to tell you where they were headed," added Jack. "Ride Magic along the creek and you'll soon catch up. By the way, that horse should have been born a fish, the way he loves the water."

"Cool!" Grabbing her favourite straw Stetson that she'd brought with her, Kami jumped up from the table. "Thanks."

Jack and Lizzie smiled. "This is your chance to do your own thing," Lizzie insisted. "You've worked hard - you deserve it."

Jack was right - Magic was totally at home in water.

He stepped into the clear, fast-running creek and was soon up to his belly so that Kami had to raise her feet out of the stirrups to stop her boots getting wet. She laughed as Magic waded on towards an island covered in thick willows.

"How cool is this!" she sighed.

Clunk! Magic's hoof kicked a submerged rock. The rock dislodged, then grated against another.

"Whoa!" Kami clung to the saddle horn as her horse

lurched sideways, then righted himself.

Magic glanced round, as if to say, *Do you fancy a swim?*

Kami laughed. "Let's get to that island up ahead and see if we can find the girls."

Kicking him on, she looked ahead and saw that she and Magic were on the right track.

"Hey, sleepy head!" Hayley and Cool Kid emerged from the bushes. "Good rest? Alisa said you were still snoring when she left." She held up a brown paper package. "You want to share my lunch?"

"Sure." Kami was glad to catch up with them, and so was Magic, who snickered a friendly greeting to the brown-and-white Paint.

Up ahead, Alisa led Diabolo clear of the willows and waved at Kami.

"Kellie couldn't make it," Alisa explained as Magic reached the island and Kami dismounted. "She and Dylan are auditioning for a TV director. They want him to play dead for an old-style shoot-out scene between a girl on horseback and a no-good cattle rustler."

"All in a day's work at Stardust Stables," Hayley grinned. She opened up her sack lunch and offered

Kami a bag of chips and a cheese sandwich. "And here's an apple for your horse," she added.

Magic spotted the treat and his nostrils twitched. He craned his neck towards Kami's palm, grabbing the apple between his teeth and crunching loudly.

"Pretty perfect, huh?" Hayley said, as Kami sat down on the grass and gazed down the length of the creek. "Especially without the boys hassling us."

Kami nodded. Being out with just the girls made her feel totally chilled.

Water gurgled over the smooth stones and parted and gushed round the sides of pink granite boulders rising from the water. Meadow flowers grew along the banks – yellow spears of Indian tobacco plants, red poppies and blue columbines. Above their heads a strong sun hung in a pure blue sky, promising another scorching day ahead.

Kami smiled to herself. This was the life! She was sitting with great new friends in a beautiful setting. And sure, the riding was challenging and the tricks were dangerous, but she had the best little stunt horse in the world by her side.

"So you're over being homesick and you're going to

stay the whole six weeks?" Alisa checked.

Kami swallowed and nodded. "I'm going to learn every stunt in the book," she promised. "And if Jack and Lizzie ask me, Magic and I are going to audition for *Moonlight Dream.*"

"You're a good fit," Alisa assured her. "You could be Coreen's twin."

"More than Becca," Hayley added. "But don't tell her I said that!"

"Becca would definitely want that gig," Alisa commented. "But she's a little bit too tall and too old to double for Coreen."

Again Kami nodded. "I'll keep my fingers crossed."

Hayley grinned. "Right! Just that one job would solve the current Stardust cash-flow problem."

"Until the next crisis," Alisa pointed out with a sigh. "Seriously, Kami, you could totally do it. You look exactly right, which none of the rest of us do, and you've sure got the guts and the talent, so forget about Becca maybe wanting the same gig. Just go out there and win it – we'll be right behind you."

"OK, if it happens, I'll do it," Kami vowed as they finished their lunch and climbed back into the saddle.

She and Magic led the way into the creek. "Hey, I'm glad I caught up with you guys. This is fun."

"Likewise." Hayley brought Cool Kid alongside, with Alisa and Diabolo close behind.

"How about a lope?" Alisa suggested as they reached a stretch of smooth sand.

Kami squeezed Magic's sides and felt him surge ahead, kicking up spray as he went. Cold water splashed her and soon she was soaked from head to foot.

"Go, girl!" Hayley called from behind.

So Kami let Magic lope on through the creek, between the flower-strewn banks.

chapter three

That afternoon it was back to serious work in the round pen.

Jack had gathered the young riders at Stardust to practise vaulting on and off their horses.

"Hayley, go ahead and show the others how it's done," he instructed from his position perched on the high fence. Like Lizzie, he wore a black cowboy shirt with white piping and a black Stetson to keep the sun off his lean face.

Kami and the others gathered in the centre while Hayley swung out of the saddle and sent Cool Kid loping round the rim. The sturdy pony snorted and kicked up dirt while Hayley stood in one spot, watching him closely. After his second circuit she made her move, sprinting towards him and landing both hands flat on his broad rump, then vaulting from behind, clear into the saddle.

Wow! Kami resisted the urge to cheer and clap. She watched as Hayley loped Cool Kid on one complete circuit before she hitched herself out of the saddle and smoothly vaulted off the back of her horse. She was as supple as an Olympic gymnast, Kami thought, and she made the difficult trick look easy.

"So, Kami, you learned how to do that?" Jack checked. When she nodded, he told her to go ahead and demonstrate.

Kami took a deep breath, trying her hardest to ignore Tom and Ross's raucous calls of "Yeah! Go, Kami!"

It was way harder to focus when people were watching you, but she knew it was something she would have to learn to deal with. She stood on the spot and sent Magic off on a lope round the arena, watching the rhythm of his slow, easy stride until he passed where she stood – once and then a second time. Then she counted to three and set off after him, tucking herself in behind him, getting ready to spring up and place both hands on his hindquarters then leapfrog on to his back. But it was tricky and she mistimed it, missing her chance as Magic loped on ahead.

"Stand back, wait for him to come round one more time," Jack called.

OK, next time I'll nail it, Kami told herself. She watched Magic come past her again, and set off. She tucked in close behind, then sprang forward. This time she pulled off the tricky vault. Now all she had to do was lope with Magic for one full circuit, then vault down to the ground...

"Yeah!" Hayley called as Kami reversed the sequence and landed smoothly.

"Good job!" Tom cried.

Not perfect, but Kami smiled, letting out a huge sigh of relief.

"Now Becca, your turn," Jack called. "Do it exactly the way you did it last summer for the *River Eden* movies."

As Becca eased Pepper past Kami and Magic, Kami smiled. "Good luck," she murmured.

"Luck has nothing to do with it," Becca retorted. "We're talking skill and experience, remember."

Kami blushed. Why, oh why, did Becca have to make her feel so small?

"Don't let her get to you," Kellie said, easing Dylan

alongside Kami and Magic. "She's only doing it because she's jealous."

"Of me?" Kami was shocked.

"Yes, of you." Plain speaking as always, Kellie spelled it out for Kami. "Think about it - you two could be sisters. You have the same blonde hair and blue eyes. Sure, Becca's a bit taller and heavier, and she's one year older, which counts for a lot in this junior section of the business. But she still sees you as her main rival."

"But that's crazy," Kami protested as she watched Becca perform a perfect vault into the saddle. "She's a great rider."

"With a ton of experience as a stunt double," Kellie agreed. "But that doesn't stop her looking at you and being very afraid!" She made her voice spooky for the last two words, then she giggled. "Anyway, Kami, ask me if Dylan got the cattle-rustling job."

"Did he get the job?" Kami asked as Becca finished and Jack called for Tom and Legend.

"He did!" Kellie crowed. "We get to go on location to Texas just as soon as they finalize the date!"

"My kid sister gets to go to Texas while I stay here scooping poop!" Tom complained.

He, Zak and Kami were shovelling poop, ready for Jack to drive it out to the dung heap at the far end of the meadow. Ross, Kellie and Alisa were checking tack while Becca chalked names on to the board for horses who needed new shoes.

"How come we get the worst job. Again!" Tom made a big deal of the smelly task, but only to raise a smile from Kami, who worked happily beside the boys.

"Dude, no whining!" Zak warned. "Remember, me and Ziggy almost got sent to Montana for the *Drifter* movie, until Lizzie's ex got a kid from High Noon in there instead. But do I feel bitter?"

"Yep," Tom grunted, still grinning at Kami as he raised then tipped an extra-heavy load.

"OK, so I wish I was in Montana; who wouldn't?" Zak stopped raking to lift his hat and wipe his brow with the back of his hand. "From what I hear, Pete Mason went in with a lower deal and these days it's money that does the talking. But the kid who got the job can hardly do even the simplest stuff. I saw him once at my local rodeo. Dude, he was totally unimpressive."

"Are we done here?" Tom asked, loading the final shovelful on to the trailer. "Cos if we are, there's a bale of alfalfa ready to go out to the meadow."

Wearily Kami laid down her shovel and headed for the barn with Zak and Tom. She glanced at her watch and saw that there was still an hour to go before supper.

"Not wimping out, are we?" Tom challenged with his ready grin.

"No!" Taking a swipe at him with her straw hat, Kami ran ahead. "Race you!"

They reached the barn door together, but Tom shoved her sideways against a stack of straw bales, meaning that he was first to reach the tractor loaded with alfalfa for the horses. He jumped up behind the wheel.

Covered in straw and breathless from her sprint across the yard, Kami let Zak climb up beside Tom. "You two go," she told them. "I'll stay here and give Magic some grain."

"You spoil that horse!" Tom called as he trundled the tractor out of the barn to deliver supper to the horses waiting at the meadow fence.

"Sure I do," she admitted. She went to the grain store

and scooped the small pellets into a bucket. Then she walked towards the stall where Magic was waiting. "Supper!" she announced, tipping the grain into the manger.

Magic snickered, raising his head and curling back his top lip in what looked like a smile.

Her horse fed, and craving a bit of alone-time, Kami headed for the tack room. She'd just fetched Magic's bridle when she overheard Lizzie in the middle of a phone call.

"OK, Matt, thanks. Really, thanks for trying." There was a pause, then she spoke again. "I might have known my ex would undercut us. These days the director and the head wrangler don't care so much about the quality of the riding – it's all down to money. Anyway, Pete's done this before... Yeah, I hear you... Yeah, you'll remind Brad that we're just down the road. That'd be good. Bye."

Lizzie sighed as she came off the phone. When she spotted Kami she shook her head. "It looks like the *Moonlight Dream* contract has slipped through our fingers, worse luck."

Kami frowned, but what could she say?

"Hey, not your problem," Lizzie said more cheerfully. She took the bridle out of Kami's hands and pointed her towards the door. "Magic's tack is already super-clean," she insisted. "Look – it's totally gleaming. So go in and relax."

"Sideways or back vault?" Tom asked.

It was early next morning and Kami had ridden Magic bareback into the round pen to practise her vaults. It was only 8 a.m. and she'd been surprised that Tom and Legend had beaten her in there.

"Back." She decided this was the trick she still wanted to perfect.

"You want me to comment?"

Kami nodded. "Just don't make fun of me, OK?"

"Me!" Tom swung down out of the saddle and tethered his palomino to the fence, folding his arms across his chest, ready to judge Kami's vault. "OK. Look at my face, I'm deadly serious."

"Now you're putting me off," Kami complained as

she set Magic off at a steady lope.

"Better get used to an audience. Think of all the guys on a movie set - actors, techies, director..."

"Enough already!"

As Magic galloped twice round the pen, Kami forgot about Tom and focused on her back vault. She'd learned yesterday that in this trick, timing was everything. She waited for her horse to pass her a third time, then she set off at a run, catching him up and raising both arms to place her palms flat on his rump. Smoothly she vaulted on to his back.

Magic loped on, steady as a rock.

"Good boy!" Kami murmured, leaning forward to pat his dappled neck. Then she drew him to a halt next to Tom. "Well?" she asked breathlessly.

He looked up at her with a twinkle in his grey eyes. "Work hard and you'll be..." There was a pause, then his face broke out in the biggest grin this side of the Rockies. "...the best stunt rider at Stardust!"

The best! Kami laughed, then trotted Magic on. As they passed the gate she saw two strangers walking across the parking lot to watch. Remembering Tom's advice not to let an audience distract her, she and

Magic carried on with a vaulting dismount, followed by a second vault, but this time from a sideways angle. Then she rode up, close to the visitors, the wind flapping at her plaid shirt and tugging at her hair.

"Who's this?" she heard one of the guys ask Tom as he pointed in her direction.

"That's Magic and Kami. Kami's new."

"She sure looks right," the other guy commented to his companion.

Suddenly Kami realized these visitors might be important and she slowed Magic to a trot.

"Hey, my name's Brad Morley," the first guy announced as they trotted by.

Kami recognized the name of the famous movie director and gulped. She reined Magic back, then vaulted smoothly off his back.

"I'm taking time out from the desk part of my job," the director explained. "Scott, our head wrangler on *Moonlight Dream*, is busy with another job, so I invited Matt and a couple of other actors from the movie to come scouting for talent with me. We were heading down the road to High Noon Stables, but Matt here told me we should come take a look at Stardust first,"

Brad Morley continued. "Now I want you young riders to prove that we're not wasting our time."

After that, it was all action. Lizzie and Jack hurried out of the ranch house to greet their guests. Tom ran off to round up as many Stardust horses and riders as he could muster from the corral. Soon Alisa and Diabolo, Zak and Ziggy, and Becca and Pepper had joined Kami and Magic in the round pen.

"I'm trying to convince Brad that the cheapest deal isn't always the best," Matt explained to Jack after the two had shaken hands. They watched as Lizzie made the rest of the introductions.

The director, who was small and bald, with heavy-rimmed glasses, nodded at each of the riders, but looked nervous around horses. "Actually, we're looking for two stunt doubles for *Moonlight Dream*," he explained to Lizzie. "A boy and a girl. I need to get it exactly right in terms of riding ability and physical similarity to our leading actors."

"We'd be happy to show you a few basic stunts," Lizzie told him eagerly. "Then you can judge for yourself if we can give you the right combination."

Turning to the gathered horses and riders, Lizzie gave them all an encouraging smile. "Don't be nervous," she told them. "Keep your focus and trust your horse. And most importantly, have fun!"

Oh, Jeez! Kami put her arm round Magic's neck. This was her first audition and it had come much sooner than she'd expected. Beside her, Becca stood cool as a cucumber with the sun shining prettily on her long blonde hair. Beyond them, Zak followed Lizzie's instruction to break away from the group and demonstrate a couple of stunts on Ziggy.

"Give us a spin-the-horn, then go straight into a front wing," she told him.

Zak nodded and eased Ziggy into a trot. The Appy held steady as Zak placed his palms flat on the saddle horn, took his weight all the way forward on to his hands, then executed a complete turn, like a gymnast on a pommel horse. With hardly a second to regain his breath, he then clutched the horn with his right hand and flung himself out of the saddle towards Ziggy's head.

By the fence, Matt applauded and Brad nodded his approval. "What about the kid who was riding the grey in here when we first arrived?" the director asked. Kami felt a quick jolt of disappointment as the director glanced at the riders and picked Becca and Pepper out of the group. "There you are, honey. Let me take another look at you."

"It wasn't Bec–" Tom began, but a fiery glance from Becca stopped him.

Unaware of the error, Jack talked up their experienced rider, who quickly set Pepper off from a standing start into full gallop. "Becca's a seasoned stunt rider. She worked on *River Eden* and *Gold Rush*."

Brad Morley nodded and watched with interest.

"OK, Becca, go for a one-foot drag!" Lizzie called.

Becca nailed the athletic stunt perfectly, flinging herself from the saddle and allowing herself to be dragged in the dirt for five strides before kicking her foot free of the stirrup. She jumped to her feet, then picked up her hat and dusted herself down.

Standing on the sidelines, Kami watched with a sinking heart as Brad Morley clapped and Becca gathered up Pepper's reins before walking back towards the group. As she came to a stop, she looked Kami in the eye. It was a look that said, *Beat that, newbie!*

"It's going well so far," Matt confided in Jack as the director took out a camera and snapped some close-up shots of Becca and Pepper. "My guess is that Brad will want to audition a couple more riders here before we move on to High Noon."

"Is he visiting any other stables, besides these two?" Lizzie asked anxiously.

"No," Matt assured her. "We fly back to California the day after tomorrow, to carry on filming. This is a kind of working vacation for us. Hey, if you glance over your shoulder to see who's getting out of the car, I'd say the excitement of our visit is about to kick up a gear."

All eyes swivelled towards the yard where Brad Morley's black SUV was parked. Two figures stepped out, both wearing dark glasses, both incredibly glamorous. The boy was tall and skinny, dressed in a loose white cotton shirt over dark denims and bright red Converse trainers. The girl was blonde and in Western dress – white leather jacket, fringed and studded, plus Wranglers and fancy, Cuban-heeled cowboy boots.

"Would you look at that!" Alisa sighed, her gaze fixed on the handsome face behind the Ray-Bans.

"That," said Becca, "is Nathan Atwood." For once,

even she seemed impressed.

"And Coreen Kessler!" Tom added. If he'd been a cartoon, a string of shiny red love hearts would have pulsated out of his chest. "I'm in lurve!" he gasped.

"Hey, guys, hurry on over here," Brad called.

Nathan and Coreen picked up speed to join the director, while Kami stood next to Magic, feeling as if she wanted to fade into the background.

"Are you glad you came along for the ride?" Matt asked them.

Nathan nodded "Hey, y'all." His southern drawl broke the hushed silence. "Dude, I couldn't stay in the car a minute longer. I just love your horse," he told Tom, giving Legend a stroke down the length of his nose. Then he picked out Alisa and asked her how long she'd been stunt riding and whether she got any time off for socializing.

"Hey." Coreen looked at no one in particular. She didn't reach out to any of the horses. She just stood in her white jacket, fringes swaying, studs gleaming, dazzling everyone with her perfect smile.

"They may be big names in the movies and starring in a multi-million-dollar teen romance," Brad confided in

Lizzie and Jack, "but neither of these kids have ever ridden a horse in their lives before."

Jack stepped in quickly. "You want us to give them a few basics?"

Brad nodded. "Why not, since they're here and they'll have to sit on a horse for a few location shots? Matt told me on the drive over that you guys are good teachers. And I trust his judgement on horsemanship."

"Come and get fitted for saddles," Lizzie said to Coreen and Nathan. "Tom and Alisa, fetch Sugar and Liberty from the meadow. "We'll soon have you up in the saddle and looking like you were born to ride!"

chapter four

"It sounds crazy," Lizzie told Nathan Atwood as he sat on Liberty for the very first time. "But the way to ride a horse well is to learn how to think like a horse."

Nathan looked confused. "Run that by me one more time," he muttered.

Lizzie smiled up at him. "The key is to recognize his way of looking at the world," she explained. "A horse in his natural life belongs to a large herd. That means he doesn't like being out there alone because the prairie, the mountains, or the desert, is full of hidden dangers. If you're on his back and asking him to separate off from his buddies, he has to learn to trust you big time."

"I hear you." Nathan was relaxed in the saddle, and Kami and the other riders from Stardust Stables could see that he was a natural. He didn't grip the reins too tight or press the bit against the horse's tongue, and he didn't tense up when Lizzie let go of the reins, and let Liberty step forward across the round pen.

"Good job," Lizzie called.

"He looks cool in Tom's cowboy boots," Alisa whispered to Kami. "And Ross's Stetson fits him just right."

"Anyone would look cool on Liberty," Becca pointed out. The dark bay gelding's coat shone like velvet and he held his head high and proud.

"Don't be picky," Alisa sighed. "Leave me be and let me worship the ground Nathan Atwood walks on!"

Meanwhile, Jack tried to persuade Coreen to ride Sugar. "She's real safe," he explained. "Once you understand the basic rules you'll do just fine."

But Coreen frowned and shook her head. "I paid a fortune for this jacket and these boots. I don't want to get them messed up."

"You don't want to ride?" Jack checked.

"Not right now," Coreen confirmed, then she wandered back to the car.

"Hey, Coreen, this horse feels fine," Nathan called to

her as she walked away. "You want to try him?"

Again she shook her head.

"I rarely came across a horse who wasn't fine, once the rider understands the basic rules," Lizzie said, tilting Nathan's heels down and his toes up, then adjusting the reins a little. She walked them on, keeping a steady hand on Legend's head collar. "Watch Legend's ears. If they're flicked round towards you like they are now, it means he's paying attention, waiting for you to tell him the next thing."

"How do I do that?" At ease in the saddle, Nathan was ready for more.

"If you want him to keep on walking straight ahead, squeeze with both legs - good. Keep your heels down, hold your balance, don't let your shoulders go up - well done!"

"It's a pity Coreen doesn't want to have a go," Tom said to Zak as he leaned against the fence in bare feet. "I'd give her horse-riding lessons any time she likes - for free!"

"Dream on!" Zak laughed.

"So, what do you think?" While Lizzie worked with Nathan, Matt took Brad aside for a private conversation, but they were close enough to Kami for her to catch snippets of their conversation.

"Great little rider ... grey horse ... but we'd have to hammer out a deal," she heard Brad say.

"Talk to Lizzie and Jack," Matt advised. "These are good people and they know their horses ... I've worked with Jack, way back."

The director looked at his watch. "We still have to look at Pete Mason's riders," he reminded Matt. "Tell Jack we'll come back tomorrow." Taking his phone from his pocket, he walked swiftly towards his car, head down and talking fast.

Meanwhile, inside the pen, Nathan was feeling confident enough to try his first trot.

"Sit firm in the saddle," Lizzie advised. "You need to feel like your butt is superglued to the leather."

"His butt!" Alisa echoed, sighing and faking a fainting fit.

Kami propped her upright while Becca shot her a warning glance.

"What?" Alisa protested. "If you think I'm bad, what about Tom and Zak – they couldn't take their eyes off Coreen!"

"Honestly, you'd think they'd never met a movie star in their whole lives," Becca said scornfully. "We're always working with famous actors at Stardust – what's the big deal?" Then her gaze fell on Kami. "Oh, except you," she added. "I forgot you only just got here."

Two inches high again, and groaning inwardly, Kami didn't argue. *Face it – Becca stole my spot*, she thought, leaning her head against Magic's neck. *I never got the chance to do a proper audition so if anyone gets this job, it's going to be her.*

Magic turned his head and softly nuzzled her hand.

"Oops!" Alisa's voice burst Kami's sad bubble.

Nathan had just misjudged a bend and taken his first involuntary dismount. He lay in the dirt, laughing. It seemed a movie star was only human – he fell from his horse just like everyone else.

"Why so quiet?" Hayley was the first to join Kami at supper and ask her what was the matter. She sat down next to Kami, then beckoned for Alisa and Kellie to join them.

"No reason. I'm cool." Kami tried to sound cheerful,

but who was she kidding? Inside she was still smarting from the injustice of seeing Becca being picked for the trial, when she hadn't been given a shot.

In fact, she was so upset she hardly noticed the arrival of Alisa and Kellie.

"So, you're not eating your steak, you've barely said a single word since Brad Morley drove out of here, and you still reckon there's not a problem?" Hayley persisted.

"Yeah, Kami, spill," Kellie urged. Tonight her wavy brown hair was caught up in a high ponytail and she wore a denim jacket over her plaid shirt.

"Tom told me what happened in the round pen earlier today," Alisa said.

"What did happen?" Kellie and Hayley demanded.

Alisa lowered her voice. "Becca took the credit for some vaults that Kami and Magic performed in front of Brad Morley. Tell them, Kami."

But Kami shook her head. "He made a mistake. He thought I was Becca – end of."

Alisa shook her head. "Kami didn't even get the chance to audition," she told the others.

"But Becca did?" Kellie got it at last.

Kami nodded. "And she's a great rider. What chance do I have now?"

"From what I heard on the grapevine, there's no decision until Brad comes back for a second look tomorrow morning," Kellie pointed out. "That means he must want to do more auditions."

Alisa raised a hand to bring an end to the speculation. "Kami, there are a few things you need to understand about being at Stardust Stables. Number one, we're all great riders. That's not arrogant, that's a fact. Number two - and this is important - we're all of us competing for jobs, one against the other."

"Yeah; we're friends, but we're also rivals," Kellie agreed. "Just two weeks back, Alisa and Hayley were up for the same role in a movie called *Wild Mustang*. They both went to audition out in California. Alisa got the job, Hayley didn't. Alisa did three days' filming in the desert while Hayley schlepped back here with Cool Kid. But you don't see them fighting over it, do you?"

Kami shook her head.

"That's the way it is."

"And we're not *afraid* to compete," Alisa concluded.

"What I'm saying is, you and Becca are definitely both up for the Coreen Kessler stunt-double role, just as soon as you register on Brad Morley's radar. Anyone with half a brain can see that. You look the same as Coreen, you both ride brilliantly..."

"But–" Kami began.

"No buts!" Hayley broke in. "You only have to get one thing inside your head and it's this – if you're lucky enough to go up against Becca for this role, you don't think twice – you go, girl!"

They made it sound so easy, Alisa, Kellie and Hayley. But for Kami it was more complicated. For a start, she couldn't clear her head of Becca's sneaky put-downs. And second, she had another bout of homesickness.

"You seem a little down," her mom had said when Kami had called her straight after supper.

"I'm good," Kami had told her.

"Sure?"

"Yeah, so quit worrying."

"Well, we're all good here, too. Columbine's doing well on the guest string. Your dad brought in three new horses from the stock show over in Clearwater. There's a little brown-and-white Paint that you're just going to love."

"Cool."

"And guess what – Squeaky's pregnant! We think the kittens will arrive later this month. We won't name them until you get back."

"Wow, that's great. I'm sad I won't see them born, though."

"So, what's your news, honey? Did you learn any more stunts?"

"Yeah, and today I met my first famous movie star – two, actually. Coreen Kessler and Nathan Atwood came to the stables."

"Oh, Kami!" Her mom had been really excited for her. "You must be over the moon. Is there any chance you'll actually get to work with them?"

★★★★★

"I wanted to say no," Kami admitted to Magic as she walked in the moonlight with him. She'd come straight out to the meadow after the phone call to tell him how she felt. "I wanted to ask Mom to let me come home, forget all about stunt riding and let me ride Columbine out on the trails and be there when Squeaky has her kittens."

Magic walked beside her, his hooves brushing through the lush green grass. The moon cast a silver light on to his pale grey coat.

"No offence to you," Kami told him, stopping to put an arm round his neck before they walked on together. "But instead I told Mom there was still a slim chance that I'd get to work on *Moonlight Dream* and she sounded so ... proud!" Kami sighed. She had to bite her lip to stop it from trembling. "So, even though I'm homesick, I've decided to stay and cowboy up."

Magic trod steadily on, his tail swishing, dark eyes gleaming.

"With you," Kami added. "I told Mom how brilliant you are, how we loped through the creek and you never put a foot wrong. And I said for her not to worry because you and I had built this trust between us and you'd never put me in any danger."

Magic stopped by the creek to nuzzle her arm.

"I'm right, aren't I?"

He threw back his head as if to say, *Totally. No*

question. One hundred per cent.

"So, that was it, I made my decision," she announced, looping her arms round Magic's neck. "Tomorrow we take on Becca and Pepper. We'll show the whole world what we can do!"

chapter five

"Ta-dah, we're back, you crazy, stunt-riding people!" Nathan Atwood burst into the dining room while everyone was eating breakfast. All the girls swooned and sighed over their crispy bacon and eggs over-easy as he made his way around the room, high-fiving everyone and demanding to know when he next got to ride the cool black horse.

"Dark bay," Hayley told him, seemingly the only one not to be lost for words at the appearance of the movie star. "Liberty's a dark bay. He's Jack's horse, so he's the guy to ask."

Coreen Kessler glided into the room behind him, but instead of saying hello, she kept her head down, busily checking text messages on her phone.

"They're back!" Kami echoed Nathan's words.

"That means Brad Morley really does want to take a second look at us."

"There's the man himself." Alisa pointed through the window to where the director stood in the yard with Matt, Jack and Lizzie.

"What happens now?" Kami whispered. She felt her stomach twist itself into a knot.

"It looks like Lizzie is definitely setting up more auditions," Kellie said, as Jack headed towards the ranch house.

"OK, Kami, get ready to impress. I'm sure they'll want to see you," Hayley predicted. "I wonder who they'll choose to double up for Nathan."

The knot in Kami's stomach grew tighter still. But she'd sworn to Magic last night that she would give this her best shot and that was what she planned to do – if Lizzie put her up for the audition ... and that was still a big "if".

As Jack came through the swing doors into the dining room, everyone turned and held their breath. He looked around at their faces – some eager and excited, some nervous, and some resigned to the fact that they weren't even in the running. "Good news," he announced.

"Thanks to my buddy, Matt Harrison, we're in with a real chance of sealing the *Moonlight Dream* deal. Brad didn't find anyone to fit the bill at High Noon, so now he's back here to set up official auditions. He wants to see two possible contenders for Coreen's stunt double and two for Nathan's."

"Good job!" a couple of kids called out.

"Lizzie and I have decided who we want to put forward." Jack let the tension mount, speaking slowly and walking between the tables until he got a good view of everyone gathered there. "The two boys who will be auditioning today are..."

Kami groaned inwardly. Jeez, this was worse than the *X Factor* results!

"...Ross and Tom!" Jack declared.

There were whoops and cheers as the two boys stood up, ready to go out and saddle up their horses.

"And the two girls are..."

Kami gripped the edge of the table until her knuckles turned white. She swallowed hard.

"...Becca and Kami!"

"Go, Becca! Go, Kami!" The shout went up as kids banged the tables with their cutlery.

The noise almost deafened Kami as she stood up. Hayley grinned, Alisa and Kellie nodded their encouragement. "You can do it!" they mouthed.

Across the room, Kami watched Becca scrape back her chair. Her rival brimmed with confidence as she high-fived her neighbour, then went up to Coreen. "Come and watch," she invited as if they were already best buddies.

"Ready, Kami?" Jack called above the noise and general excitement. "Let's go."

Kami's legs wobbled as she crossed the room and by the time she reached the porch she felt totally light-headed. But it was now or never, so, setting her wide-brimmed straw Stetson low on her forehead to cut out the bright sun, she strode towards the corral.

"This is it!" Kami told Magic. She was brushing every last speck of dirt out of his coat and each tiny tangle out of his mane and tail.

Magic stood with ears pricked, his attention fixed on Tom as he rode Legend into the round pen. Ross followed behind on his horse, Jack D, or Dee for short

– a light sorrel the colour of the famous whisky.

Kami grinned. "I know, you want us to get out there so you can see how they do. I'm working as fast as I can."

At the rail next to theirs, Becca had already tightened Pepper's cinch and was checking the length of her stirrups. By the entrance to the round pen, Brad stood chatting with Matt and Jack while Lizzie instructed the boys on the stunts she wanted them to perform.

"OK, time to get your saddle on," Kami told Magic. She heaved the heavy tack into position, then fastened the girth loosely. "Now for your bridle."

Magic lowered his head to let her slide the bit between his teeth. He stood patiently as she adjusted the straps.

"Ready?" Kami asked as she eased his forelock over the brow band.

Magic gave a low snort and stamped his foot impatiently.

Beside them Becca swung nimbly into her saddle. "Let's go kick ass," she told Pepper.

"Uh-oh, cinch," Kami muttered to herself,

remembering to stoop and make the final check. She tightened the thick strap under Magic's belly by a couple of holes before she was satisfied. "OK, now we're all set. Let's go."

Ross was first up.

"We want to see Dee rear up and paw the air," Lizzie told him. "After that, we want him to crow hop across the pen, going into a full bucking session over by the far rail. You got that?"

Ross nodded. He looked relaxed in front of his audience, leaning forward to pat Dee, then walk him on a full circuit before he began the stunts.

"I'm not sure we want a plain brown horse," Brad muttered uncertainly to Matt and Jack. "Aren't they a little boring?"

"Dee has plenty of character," Jack explained. "Just you watch!"

With a subtle shift of weight, Ross asked his horse to rear up on his hind legs. The little sorrel pawed the air, his chestnut mane flung back. Then he was down and arching his back, bouncing up from the ground off all four legs, while Ross raised his hat and waved it in the air like an old-time rodeo cowboy.

"Crow hopping," Jack informed the director. "And now bucking."

Ross used new pressure to make Dee plunge his head down and kick his back legs out. The rider rocked forward, then back, as Dee landed, then forward again as the spirited sorrel threw in an extra buck.

"Whoa!" Lizzie called the display to a halt. "Thanks, Ross - good job. Now Tom - your turn."

Kami waited with Magic by the gate and watched Tom make a last adjustment to his stirrups as he took instructions from Lizzie. Legend looked great. Palominos were such pretty horses, with their honey-coloured coats and blond manes and tails. She felt sure that Brad would be impressed. Tom looked great in the saddle, too, she noted with a blush.

"Tom will start with a front wing," Lizzie told the director. "That means he hangs on to the saddle horn with one hand, throws himself out of the saddle and flings himself forward. Keep an eye on Legend - her strong point is her stamina."

Brad nodded. "I need these horses to race along a

beach for a big scene in the movie. Stamina would be good."

As Tom set Legend off at a lope, then flung himself forward out of the saddle, Kami could see the work the horse was putting in, holding her balance and keeping up her pace as her rider threw himself around. She saw patches of sweat appear as white foam on her honey-gold neck, but still Legend loped on round the pen.

"OK, Tom, finish with a double vault," Lizzie called.

No sooner said than Tom vaulted out of the saddle to one side, then back up again and out to the other. Finally he vaulted into the saddle and reined his horse to a halt. Meanwhile, Lizzie got Becca and Pepper ready for their audition.

"Becca, I want you to show Brad some Roman riding. That means, Kami, you'll ride Magic alongside Pepper and be prepared for Becca to stand and transfer her weight so that she straddles both horses. You got that?"

Kami nodded and eased Magic into position.

"Don't mess this up," Becca warned quietly.

"We won't," Kami promised. Other kids might have been tempted, but not her. She wanted this to be a fair competition, no dirty tricks.

The two riders set off side by side, their horses keeping perfect time.

"Good boy, Magic," Kami breathed as she sat quiet in the saddle while Becca stood nimbly on Pepper's back. Becca stood with arms stretched wide, flexing her legs to absorb her horse's movement. When she stepped across to straddle the two horses and Magic felt her weight on his rump, he didn't falter. "Good, good boy!"

"Thanks, Kami, thanks, Becca!" Lizzie called. When the stunt was complete and Becca was back on her own horse, she called Kami and Magic back to the gate while Becca finished off her display with a couple of vertical wings and a final dramatic saddle fall.

"And last but not least, Kami and Magic," Lizzie told Brad, while both Nathan and Coreen congratulated Becca on her audition.

"Is this the kid we saw yesterday, when we first got here?" the puzzled director asked Matt, looking from Kami to Becca and back again.

It was Tom who shot in with an answer. "Yeah, Kami and Magic – that's who you saw," he confirmed.

Kami smiled her thanks and tried not to tighten up.

Shoulders down, breathe easy, relax.

"Let's have a few vaults," Lizzie told her. "Any sequence you like. Then spin the horn and vault out of the saddle to finish."

OK, we can do this! Kami thought to herself. She gathered her courage and felt Magic eager to go. Stepping out of the saddle, she clicked her tongue and set him off at a lope, clockwise round the pen. He circled once and as he passed her, nostrils flared and nearside ear flicked towards her, she sprinted after him and with one bound she vaulted into the saddle.

Magic flicked both ears back towards her, then loped on.

Kami felt his strength, his smoothness, his total confidence. This horse lived up to his name - he was magic and he would never let her down. She forgot the onlookers and began to enjoy herself - out of the saddle and running alongside, back up again with more strength in her arms and legs than she ever knew she had. Out again on the far side and sprinting, laughing as she vaulted back into the saddle.

Magic didn't falter or put a foot wrong. He and his new stunt rider were as one.

"Ready for our finale?" Kami murmured. "Spin the horn."

For this, the most difficult stunt, she put her weight forward on to the hand resting on the saddle horn, then alternated hands as she twisted and scissored her legs across Magic's back and over his neck, and again until she'd turned full circle.

"Again!" she told him, adding an even faster spin. "And one last time." At the end of the third spin she vaulted clear.

Magic slowed down and let her jog beside him. They came to a halt in front of the director and his two young stars.

"Good job, everyone. You kids are far and away the best stunt riders we've seen so far. But now for the hard part." Brad Morley didn't waste time when it came to casting decisions. He turned first to Ross and Jack D. "Son, I like the way you ride and I'll keep you on my list for future work, no doubt about it." Then he turned to Tom. "But you're the same height as Nathan and the same skinny build, plus Lizzie assures me your horse has enough stamina to race along a beach in California for however many takes we need."

"She sure does," Tom said, looping an affectionate arm round Legend's neck.

"So you get the job as Nathan Atwood's stunt double," Brad decided.

"Hey, partner!" Nathan gave Tom a high five, then told Ross he was a cool rider anyway. "Another time, dude," he added.

Meanwhile, it was time for Brad Morley's next choice. "Now for the girls. This sure is hard," he admitted, looking down to check through his notes.

Kami took a deep breath, then held it. Becca's chin was up and she was smiling, looking super-confident.

"Becca, your resumé is impressive – all your past work, your current level of skill. And Kami, you're new so your record is unproven..."

Kami's heart sank. Brad would go for experience, for Becca's proven track record.

"However, that's not a major problem," the director continued. "You're both excellent riders. No, my decision here rests on one issue." He paused and seemed to think deeply. "Let me ask you, Lizzie. We have three scenes to shoot on an open beach, so which one of these horses will work best in that situation?"

Lizzie looked from Magic to Pepper, then back again. Kami still held her breath.

"That would be Magic," Lizzie said slowly. "He's great around water."

Magic's head was up, as if he knew he was being praised. Becca turned away, trying to hide her disappointment.

Brad Morley smiled and came forward to shake Kami's hand. "Then the job of Coreen Kessler's stunt double goes to you and Magic," he confirmed. "Pack your bags – you're flying out to California the day after tomorrow!"

chapter six

Kami hardly knew that Sunday had happened.

She remembered calling home with the good news and her dad yelling for her mom to come to the phone to hear the words straight from Kami's mouth. "Heather, Kami's going to California!" She'd heard him shout out across the yard where new guests were arriving at Elk Creek. "Our daughter got a stunt-riding job!"

The rest of the day was a blur of laundry and packing, drinking soda with Hayley, Kellie and Alisa, taking apples to Magic in the meadow and listening to last-minute instructions from Lizzie.

"Jack will fly out to Santa Barbara with you," she'd explained. "The horses will travel on the same plane – all at the movie company's expense. Don't look so worried. Our horses are used to plane journeys and there's no time to trailer them out all the way to Califonia."

Kami had been too excited to take in any details, but she could see the relief in Lizzie's face as she and Jack discussed the finer details of the plans.

"Happy?" Tom had asked her as he joined her in the laundry with a ton of last-minute washing. "You went up against Becca and won."

"Don't I know it," Kami'd said. "She's not said a word to me since."

"Don't worry about Becca," Tom had reassured her. "The important thing is, are you happy?"

"Scared, more like," she'd admitted. "This is such a big deal."

Dropping his dirty laundry on the floor, Tom had dragged Kami over to the cold drinks machine and sat her down under the yellow umbrella. "So what's scaring you?" he'd asked.

"Everything." The distance they had to travel, meeting the film crew, trying not to make a fool of herself by messing up the stunts... Yeah, everything!

"You're sitting here, wondering if you can do this," Tom had guessed. The twinkle didn't leave his eyes as he shrugged and said, "Me, too."

"No - really?" She hadn't believed him. "You've done this a dozen times."

"And each time I'm more scared than the time before, believe me."

"No!" He was only saying this to help her.

"Yeah." He'd leaned forward, elbows on the table, cradling his Coke can between his hands. "But you know what I do? I focus on Legend. I think about her and nothing else."

Kami had listened and found straight away that this made sense. Concentrate on Magic, make sure he's happy.

"Thanks, that's good advice," she'd told Tom, and she'd gone out to the meadow to take another apple to her horse.

At five thirty on Monday morning, Lizzie came into Kami and Alisa's bedroom and quietly shook Kami awake.

Kami opened her eyes. It was dark and for a few seconds she was confused.

"It's me, Lizzie. Time to go down to the meadow and

bring Magic into the corral. Tom's already up and dressed."

The idea of Tom being ready before her got Kami out of bed, dressed in jeans and T-shirt and out into the yard in a flash. Her boots crunched on the gravelled track as she fastened her jacket and glanced up at the jagged horizon where a pink gleam told her that the sun was slowly rising. Still, it was too dark to make out Tom's figure as he emerged from the barn.

"I got two head collars," he told her as she joined him. He handed one to her and they walked on in silence until they came to the meadow gate. "That's weird," Tom murmured, placing his hand on the gate and finding that it swung open. "Someone left it unbolted."

Kami couldn't see, but she could hear horses not far away, either swishing their hooves through the grass as they approached or noisily grazing. "Everything seems fine," she said.

"No, definitely weird." Tom stooped to examine the bolt. "Zak was the last person out here yesterday night – he drove the tractor loaded with alfalfa. No way would he forget to bolt the gate."

"Yeah, that is strange," Kami agreed. Then she clicked her tongue and raised her voice to call for Magic.

She expected him to snicker and come trotting up as usual, but not this morning. She clicked, called again and waited.

A horse appeared out of the pre-dawn gloom, but it was Cool Kid, not Magic – she recognized him by his brown-and-white markings, which showed clearly in the half-light. He came and nudged her uneasily with his nose, ears flattened and nostrils flared. "You're right, something weird has happened," she told Tom as alarm bells rang in her head.

"Yeah, and I can't find Legend." Tom strode across the meadow, head collar in hand. "This is not good," he muttered.

"Magic, where are you?" Kami called as Cool Kid came right up and nudged her back towards the gate. Now of all days was not the time for any of the horses to go AWOL.

Insistently, the little Paint pushed her back through the gate while Tom called for Kami to look up towards the dirt track leading out of the steep-sided valley. "I hear a truck!" he yelled.

"I can't see anything!" she yelled back, but just then a car's headlights raked across the hillside and the truck itself emerged from a stand of Lodgepole pines. Tom sprinted to join her just as the driver skidded round a final bend before vanishing out of sight.

"Jeez!" he groaned. "I didn't think even he would play such a dirty trick."

"What are you talking about?"

"I recognize the truck," he muttered. "We just had an unscheduled visit from Pete Mason."

"Lizzie's ex?"

Tom nodded. "He clearly doesn't like the fact that Lizzie and Jack won the *Moonlight Dream* contract. This must be his way of getting back at them."

"By opening the gate and letting our horses out?" It took Kami some time to figure it out, but when she did she felt a flash of anger mixed with panic. "How stupid is that! Doesn't he know it's dangerous for horses out there on the mountain!" she cried.

"Sure, he knows," Tom said grimly. "That's why he did it. It's going to be difficult to prove, though. It's our word against his."

"So why are we standing here talking?" Kami had

no idea how many Stardust horses had escaped and it was still too dark to count. What she did know was that Magic and Legend were definitely among the missing. "You go and tell Lizzie and Jack what's happened. I'll ride out and start looking."

There was no time to lose. The sun was creeping over the horizon and hitting the tops of the mountains on the west side of the valley as Kami eased the head collar on to Cool Kid and turned the lead rope into a rough version of reins. There was no bit in his mouth, but at least she had a little control as she vaulted on to his back and headed out towards the creek.

"Search in the willows!" Tom called after her as he ran to the ranch house. "And don't worry, horses see better in the dark than we do!"

"OK, Cool Kid, you know what we have to do," Kami murmured, easing the Paint horse into a lope along the bank. "We're looking for Legend and Magic, and whoever else happens to be out here."

Hayley's plucky horse picked up speed, heading along the creek until they came to the island – the girls' favourite picnic spot. Here he slowed to a walk, then raised his head to give a shrill whinny.

Silence. There was no reply from the runaway horses.

"I don't know about you, Cool Kid, but I'm thinking bad things," Kami admitted. "I'm picturing coyotes and mountain lions."

She knew from experience at Elk Creek that coyotes hunted in packs, creeping silently through shadows, tracking their prey. Mountain lions were solitary hunters with sharp claws and powerful jaws. And they were active in the pre-dawn, stalking along the ridges, seeking out vulnerable victims – a sickly calf, a wounded deer. She imagined Magic, perhaps injured and trapped down a narrow gulch, unable to escape.

Picking up the urgency in his rider's voice, Cool Kid raised his head again and listened intently.

Kami heard the wind in the trees, nothing else.

But the horse had picked up something. He turned away from the creek and sure-footedly set off up the mountain in the early morning light, crunching through loose gravel and across smooth granite rock until he came to a flat ledge and whinnied again.

This time Kami picked up a reply from higher up the slope. It was faint, but it was definitely a horse answering Cool Kid's call.

"Good job – let's go!" she murmured, squeezing the horse's sides and letting him pick his own way towards a thick stand of pine trees.

A horse whinnied as they approached the trees, but the cry was drowned out by the howl of a coyote, then another and another. The sounds sent a chill down Kami's spine.

That horse could be hurt. He could easily have broken a leg out here! She pictured the pack of wild dogs crouching low, ready to pounce.

Kami and Cool Kid entered the stand of Lodgepole pines. A cold wind rustled the pine needles and made branches creak. More coyotes joined in the blood-curdling chorus. Kami leaned forward to pat her nervous horse's neck and urge him on.

They came at last to the entrance to a narrow gulley where rocks rose sheer to either side. Cool Kid whinnied, and this time there was an answer from two or three different horses.

"Good boy!" Kami murmured, peering down the dark gulley on the lookout for the pack of grey, silent hunters blocking the exit. Then she raised her voice. "Magic, are you in there?"

There was a high, familiar whinny, and at the same time, the first shaft of sunlight hit the ridge to the west.

There they were - five or six coyotes lined up with hackles raised and staring down into the gulley. Then they spotted Kami and Cool Kid.

"Yah!" Kami yelled a warning at the top of her voice, dropping Cool Kid's lead rope and waving both hands above her head. At the same time a pale shape emerged from the gloom, followed by two others. "Magic, thank heavens you're safe!" Recognizing the lead horse, Kami slipped from Cool Kid's back and ran towards him.

Up on the ridge the disappointed coyotes began to retreat. First one, then another slipped from view.

"It's OK. Everything's OK!" Kami greeted Magic as Legend and Pepper followed him out of the gulley. Right away, Kami saw that Pepper was limping. "Good boy, you took care of Pepper," she breathed in Magic's ear. "You were scared of the coyotes, but you didn't leave him. Good, brave boy! And you, too, Legend. What happened to you, Pepper?"

Becca's horse was in so much pain that he was hardly able to put any weight on the injured leg and

Kami could see there was already a swelling on the knee joint. He was trembling and his neck and belly were covered in sweat. "It's OK," she soothed, "the coyotes have gone. Now we need to get you back home fast."

But how to get four horses down the mountain and back to the safety of the corral without any ropes or other tack? She needed help and hoped that Tom was bringing Jack and Lizzie in the right direction. "They'll follow our tracks," she told Cool Kid, sounding more certain than she felt.

The horses stood, heads raised. With one hand on Magic's neck, Kami strained to hear.

Silence, then – yes, a distant whinny from down in the valley, answered by Cool Kid, the hero of the hour. He whinnied a second time, and soon Magic and Legend joined in.

"It won't be long," Kami promised Pepper, as the horse trembled with pain. Her thoughts flew ahead. Even if they got everyone safely back to Stardust, would there still be time to get Magic and Legend loaded on the trailer, ready to fly them out to California? *If not, Pete Mason has got exactly what he wanted,* she thought.

He's wrecked the whole Moonlight Dream *deal!*

She waited and watched. Every moving shadow fooled her into thinking that help had arrived, but the minutes ticked by and the sun rose higher in the sky.

"Hurry!" she urged.

At last! Jack and Liberty were the first to appear. Kami saw the look of relief on Jack's face as he spotted them at the entrance to the gulley. "Stay right where you are," he called to Kami. "We'll be with you in five minutes."

"You hear that, Pepper?"

Becca's horse took three limping steps down the slope towards Jack, then stopped.

"She's lame," Kami called down to Jack. "There was a pack of coyotes after them. I guess she caught her foot in a crack in the rock and twisted her knee."

"Keep her right there," he instructed again as Tom appeared behind him riding Dylan, followed by Lizzie on Sugar. "And Kami, block the exit so the others can't take off again."

She did as Jack told her and soon he and Liberty made it up the mountain with head collars for the runaways. By the time Lizzie and Tom had joined him, all the horses were secure and Jack was running his hands over Pepper's swollen knee.

Now it was Lizzie's turn to make decisions. "Tom, you grab Legend's lead rope and dally her off the mountain. Likewise Kami, you ride Cool Kid and lead Magic home. Jack, I'll ride on ahead of Tom and Kami and drive the small trailer up the Jeep track to meet you, Liberty and Pepper at Snake Rock. I reckon it's about two hundred metres north from here. Do you think Pepper will make it that far?"

"I guess so," Jack agreed. He quickly checked his watch. "We have one hour to get Magic and Legend ready to trailer out to the airport," he reminded Tom and Kami. "Can we do it?"

"You bet!" they told him. They spoke as one - no way was Pete Mason's sabotage going to stop them getting on to the *Moonlight Dream* film set, on time and in good shape.

chapter seven

It was only when Kami had Magic safely tethered to a rail in the corral that she finally breathed easy.

The journey down the mountain had gone well – there had been no problem dallying Legend and Magic back to the stables, and by the time the corral was in sight Tom and Kami could see that Lizzie had already jumped into the small trailer and set off on the drive back up to Snake Rock. Still, Kami hadn't relaxed until she and Cool Kid had led Magic along the creek and into the yard.

"Hey, Kami!" Hayley ran out of the ranch house to take Cool Kid from her. "We heard what happened. Is everyone OK?"

Kami nodded. "Your horse was amazing. He tracked down the runaways."

"You bet he did!" Hayley's impish smile lit up her face. "Cool Kid, you're so smart!" she cooed as she tied him to a nearby rail and began to brush him down.

Kellie had already taken Dylan from Tom and left him to deal with Legend. "You two need to work fast," she reminded them.

"Thanks for telling me something I already knew, sis," Tom replied.

"Did someone call the vet for Pepper?" Kami asked as she started to groom Magic.

"Becca's on to it right now," Kellie answered.

As she spoke, Becca appeared on the ranch house porch, shading her eyes against the low morning sun. She glanced anxiously in the direction of Snake Rock, but she seemed nervous and held back from joining the group.

"We heard Pete Mason paid us a visit," Hayley commented.

Tom nodded. "It looks like he went into the meadow and deliberately separated Legend and Magic from the rest, then spooked them so bad they took off into the mountains. Pepper probably got mixed up in the drama by accident."

Kellie frowned as she watched Becca slowly step down from the porch. "Maybe this is my suspicious mind," she began, "but you don't think...?"

"That Becca was involved?" Hayley broke in. "Why would she be?"

"Maybe she was so eaten up by jealousy that all she could think of was to wreck the new deal. Maybe she called Mason and put the idea into his head," Kellie suggested.

But Hayley didn't sound convinced. "No way! Becca wouldn't risk her own horse!"

"Not on purpose," Kellie pointed out. "But what if Tom's right and Pepper got involved accidentally?"

Becca was now too close to the corral for them to vent any more suspicions.

As Kami ran her brush through Magic's mane, she wondered if her rival was ruthless enough to try something like that. But quickly she banished the thought from her mind.

"Hey, Becca." Hayley's tone was curt. "You talked to the vet?"

Becca walked slowly into the corral and across to the tack-room porch, where she stood in the shade.

"He's on his way," she confirmed.

Kami sneaked a look over Magic's shoulder. Becca was drained of her normal confidence; she looked all shaken up. "Try not to stress. Pepper will be back soon," she called.

"Thanks." Becca glanced at her watch, then hung her head. She seemed to think for a while, then came across and hovered close to Kami, all the time searching the Jeep track for signs of the returning trailer.

Kami reached for the protective tail bandage that Magic would wear for the long journey out to Santa Barbara. Slowly and methodically she began to bind his tail.

"So Pepper's lame?" Becca began quietly.

Kami nodded. "It looks like he sprained the ligaments in his knee."

"But it's not too bad?"

Kami glanced up, hearing the break in Becca's voice, to see tears in her eyes. "Like Jack said, fingers crossed it's nothing too serious," she reassured her. "Maybe painkillers and box rest for a couple of days."

"I feel so lousy," Becca mumbled.

Kami felt the tension in the corral mount. Hayley,

Kellie and Tom were all tuned in to their conversation.

"What've you got to feel bad about?" Hayley asked pointedly.

There was a long pause while Becca gulped back tears. "For not being there for Pepper when he needed me. It should have been me riding out to find him, not Kami."

Kami almost heard the sighs of relief from the others. "Don't beat yourself up," she consoled Becca. "Your horse is sure going to need all the TLC you can give him when he gets back to Stardust."

"I'll be there for him twenty-four seven," Becca promised. She knitted her brows and thought for a while. "So, how did they get out of the meadow in the first place?" she asked finally.

"You didn't hear about Pete Mason?" Kami checked.

Becca frowned in genuine puzzlement. "No - what about him?"

"Me and Tom, we saw him heading out of here just before dawn."

"Driving like a crazy guy," Tom confirmed without looking up or breaking the rhythm of his brushstrokes through Legend's blonde mane. "Our theory is, he was the one who unbolted the gate and drove Magic and Legend out on to the mountain. Pepper got involved because he was in the wrong place at the wrong time."

Becca shook her head and groaned. "That lousy, low-down..."

"Exactly," Kami agreed. She finished Magic's tail bandage and reached for the padded boots to protect his legs.

"We have to tell the cops." Becca spoke rapidly. "Our horses could've died. The guy should go to jail for this."

If there were still any lingering doubt in anyone's mind, Becca's flushed, angry face convinced them. No way was she faking it.

Kami nodded, then bent to strap on Magic's boots. "Easy, boy," she murmured as he shifted his weight.

"Leave it with me," Becca told her, realizing that Kami and Tom were racing against time. "I'll talk it through with Lizzie and we'll make sure Pete Mason doesn't get away with this." Then she spotted Lizzie driving the trailer back down the Jeep track and hurried off to meet her. At the corral gate she hesitated and retraced her steps. "One more thing," she whispered in a voice so low that only Kami could hear.

Kami looked up from under Magic's arched neck. "Thank you for finding Pepper."

"Honestly, it was nothing."

"No, really, Kami – thank you." Becca's face was flushed and her eyes were once more full of tears. "And I want to say sorry."

"For what?" Standing up straight, Kami looked Becca in the eye.

"For acting the way I did," Becca mumbled. "For ... you know, for being jealous and not making you feel welcome here at Stardust. For behaving badly during the auditions."

"No problem. Really." Now it was Kami's turn to feel hot and flushed. "We both really wanted that job – it was game on!"

"So, that's it – thank you and sorry," Becca insisted. "We're buddies?"

"Buddies." Slowly Kami smiled, then she grabbed Becca's arm and turned her back towards the Jeep track. "Go!" she insisted.

Becca nodded, then sprinted for the gate.

Kami took a deep breath. *Wow, that was a big*

surprise, she thought with a long, satisfied sigh. *Now all I have to do is get on that plane and prove to Brad Morley that he made the right choice when he picked me as Coreen Kessler's stunt double!*

Flying over the Rockies at 32,000 feet, Kami gazed down on endless miles of bare grey mountains broken up by dark patches of forest and thin silver rivers snaking through. From up here it looked like vast and hostile territory.

"It makes you wonder how the first settlers ever made it through to the west," she said to Tom.

"A lot died trying," he reminded her. He sat, seat tilted back, long legs stretched out into the aisle.

"This is a two-hour flight. You want to switch seats and take a look out of the window?" Kami offered.

He shook his head. "All I want is to get there."

"Me, too," Kami admitted. "How do you think Magic and Legend are doing down there in the hold?"

"They'll be doing good," Tom assured her. "Remember, this is a special equine aircraft – the stalls back there are air-conditioned and Jack's in with them."

It had been a close call - the drive to Denver International with only minutes to spare, the paperwork checks and then the loading of the horses into a hold containing other licensed stock, the hurried check-in with Jack at the departure gate. But they'd made it on to the Santa Barbara flight and had an estimated arrival time of 3.20 p.m.

"Chill," Tom advised Kami, who was fiddling with her air-con control switch. "Get some beauty sleep."

"I can't sleep on planes," she sighed. "Hey, what do you mean 'beauty sleep'? You're saying I need it?"

Tom laughed. "No, you look fine, believe me - apart from the bags under your eyes. Hah, joke! All I'm saying is, you'll want to look your best now that you get to work on set with the world's hottest screen idol."

"Nathan Atwood?"

"Who else? I saw you when he came into the ranch house that first day - you were drooling over him just like my sister and the rest."

"I was not!"

"Were."

"Was not. Anyway, what about you and Coreen Kessler?"

"Not my type," he lied.

"Oh, c'mon! You don't fool me, Coreen is everybody's type. You're telling me you alone amongst all the boys I know wouldn't kill to date her?"

Raising his eyebrows and giving a small shrug, Tom plugged in his earphones and tuned into the on-board movie. "Hey, guess who's starring!" he said, pointing to the screen at a moody, close-up shot of Nathan Atwood playing a vampire in his latest blockbuster release. "It's your new crush!"

Kami groaned and closed her eyes. It was going to be a long trip.

More paperwork on arrival meant more hanging around for Jack, Kami and Tom, so that it was late afternoon by the time they drove Magic and Legend out of Santa Barbara's airport and headed south along the coast.

"So, where are we going now?" Tom asked Jack, whose black shirt and Stetson looked out of place in the urban sprawl.

"The film crew is based at a ranch named Five Sisters,

twenty miles out of town." Jack negotiated traffic lights and followed signs for Highway 61. "Five Sisters is backed by a National Forest wilderness area and it looks out on to the Pacific Ocean."

"Where we do the beach scenes?" Kami asked.

"Right. And you're about to get thrown in at the deep end - excuse the pun," Jack told her. "Tomorrow Brad wants to shoot a big scene where Coreen's character rides her horse along the beach. It climaxes with the girl falling from her horse and getting dragged along the sand."

"Simple," Tom assured Kami. "Saddle fall followed by a drag. You can do that, no problem."

Tom was confident for her, but Kami frowned as she stared at the road ahead. It seemed just yesterday that she'd been a normal kid living on a guest ranch, riding her horse along mountain trails. Now here she was in sunny California, driving out to a movie set, discussing complicated stunts and committed to working in front of cameras and crew with actors she'd only ever seen and read about in magazines. Crazy!

"You're quiet, Kami," Jack said as the sun sank quickly over the ocean to their right. "Are you OK?"

"I'm good," she muttered. She watched the tiny figures of surfers riding the crests of waves before they crashed on to the shore. She saw miles of empty white beach ahead. "I just hope I don't let you and Lizzie down."

"You won't," Jack promised. "Just trust Magic. Listen to what he says."

"OK, Magic, this is home for the next few days."

The journey was over and Kami was introducing her horse to his accommodation at Five Sisters Ranch, a sprawling, Spanish-style set-up with white stucco buildings and red-tiled roofs.

Magic stood at the gate, looking out on to a meadow. He curled his top lip.

"I know – the grass isn't as green and lush as you're used to. It's hot here in the summer and they don't have year-round rainfall. But you get alfalfa morning and night," Kami promised.

Magic took a couple of steps into the small meadow with its white rail fences and fancy metal feeder. He glanced up at the forested hillside beyond.

"Los Padres National Forest," Kami explained. "And that sound you hear in the distance? That's the Pacific Ocean."

Still Magic hesitated, reluctant to follow Legend across the meadow.

"Go!" Kami told him as he nuzzled her arm.

Magic tilted his head, then nuzzled her again, as if checking she was certain.

"Sure!" she insisted breezily. It was dusk, but still warm enough to wear only a T-shirt and jeans. As Magic finally sauntered off to join Legend, Kami bolted the gate and walked back towards the ranch house, past giant trucks loaded with film equipment, silver trailers and SUVs, which housed the crew. A bright lamp cast yellow light along the main porch. Kami picked out Tom and Jack talking with Matt Harrison, then Brad Morley with a couple of older guys and finally, standing to one side, the unmistakable figures of Coreen Kessler and Nathan Atwood.

"Kami?" Nathan was the first to spot her as she halted by the last of the SUVs and he beckoned for her to join them. "You remember me, right?"

Swallowing hard, Kami stepped up into the porch

and nodded. "How could I not."

"Yeah, I guess," Nathan grinned. "Sorry - I'm still not used to being famous. Listen, you and Coreen need to talk."

"We do?"

"You definitely do. But don't tell Brad - OK?"

"OK," Kami agreed uncertainly. She was instantly feeling unfriendly vibes radiating from Coreen.

"Leave it, Nathan," Coreen snapped. "That was a private conversation between you and me."

"My mistake," he shrugged and gave Kami an apologetic smile as Coreen turned on her heel and disappeared into the house. "Prima donna!" he whispered, cupping his hand round his mouth.

Kami smiled. Who could resist those big brown eyes? Deep breath, be cool. "Will you be on set tomorrow?" she asked, stammering over her words and blushing madly. So not cool!

"Yeah, I just checked my schedule," Nathan replied, giving her that great smile again. Kami blushed even more.

"It's my first ever shoot," she mumbled, then gabbled on. "I guess you already knew that." *As if he cares,* she told herself with a sigh. *He's Nathan Atwood!*

He smiled – oh, that smile!

"So Kami, I have to go, they need me in the wardrobe trailer. But I'll be on the beach at eight thirty," he promised. "See you there!"

chapter eight

Kami read the script five times before breakfast. She studied the scene before and the scene after the one involving her gallop along the beach. She looked at the schedule to triple-check her 8 a.m. start.

"Jittery?" Jack asked as she went out to fetch Magic from the meadow at six thirty. He and Tom were already there, loading hay into the feeder.

"Yeah." In fact, she'd tossed and turned most of the night, rehearsing in her mind the moment on the beach when she would fling herself sideways from Magic's back, leaving one foot in the stirrup and allowing herself to be dragged for twenty metres along the ground. As usual, it would cost her a few bruises. Plus, it would need split-second timing and a total understanding between her and her horse.

"It's good to be nervous," Jack insisted. "You wouldn't be human otherwise."

Nodding, she buckled Magic's head collar and led him into a small corral behind the row of silver trailers where the actors were getting ready for the morning's scenes. A moment later, Matt emerged from the wardrobe trailer, all buttoned up in a business suit, collar and tie. He nodded at Coreen as she entered the make-up trailer next door, then came over to where Kami was grooming Magic.

"Did they give you your costume yet?"

Kami shook her head, then stood back to admire Magic's flowing dark mane and tail.

"They probably need you in the wardrobe trailer then – to check your dress size and everything."

"I better get over there, you're right!" said Kami, feeling a wave of nerves hit her. She spied Tom returning from the meadow and called for him to keep an eye on Magic. "Don't let him roll in the dirt," she said. "You hear that, Magic? No rolling!"

Her horse cocked his head to one side as if to say, *Who, me?*

Kami grinned and ran to be fitted for her costume.

Inside the trailer she met Wanda, the wardrobe mistress, who looked her up and down.

"You're Coreen's stunt double, right?"

Kami nodded. She felt excited that she was about to be dressed in the same clothes as Coreen.

"Take off your jeans and T-shirt," Wanda instructed, taking a long, pale blue dress from the rail of costumes running the length of the trailer. "Try this. You look like you're the same dress size as Coreen, so it should fit pretty well."

Wow! Kami's hands trembled a little as she put on the sleeveless, close-fitting dress. Catching sight of herself in a full-length mirror she saw that the cornflower shade of blue brought out the colour of her eyes and the shape flattered her slim figure.

"Like it?" Wanda asked.

She nodded.

"It looks good to me." Wanda gave a satisfied nod.

"Do I get shoes?" Kami asked, glancing down at her bare feet.

Wanda checked her list. "No shoes," she confirmed. "This is the romantic, shampoo-ad look." Then she took a couple of outfits from the rail, including a second pale blue dress. "Has anyone seen Coreen this morning?" she called through the open door. "I need her to get dressed."

"Still in make-up," a voice replied.

"Someone drag her out of there double quick and send her in here," Wanda insisted. "Brad's scheduled to start filming at seven. You know how he is when anyone keeps him waiting."

As a runner went to fetch Coreen, Kami stepped out of the trailer in her flowing blue dress, planning to go check on Magic one more time before Jack trailered him the short distance to the beach. Instead, she almost ran into Nathan, who sidestepped quickly and laughed at her for not looking where she was going.

"Hey, nice costume!" he added with a smile.

"Thanks," she mumbled.

"So, where's the fire?" he asked.

"No fire." She bit her lip and tried not to say anything too stupid. "We're driving Magic down to the beach. You want to come?"

Of course not. Why would drop-dead gorgeous Nathan Atwood want to drive with her in a smelly horse trailer?

"Sure. Why not?" He followed to where Jack and Tom were already loading Magic into the trailer. "Hey, Tom, don't you need to be in costume, too?"

Tom didn't seem to want to stop and chat. "Not yet," he muttered as he tethered Magic to the rail inside the trailer.

"So when do I get to shoot my scene with the 'legendary' Legend?" Nathan asked.

"That would be tomorrow," Tom told him, bolting the trailer door. "Today we get to chill."

"And you have to do all the work," Nathan said to Kami as he stood aside and let her climb into the cab before him.

She sat on the middle seat, between Jack and Nathan, trying hard not to put creases in her dress.

Jack started the engine, then paused to lean out of the driver's window and give some suggestions to Tom. "Why don't you saddle Legend and maybe ride her up into the forest? Just give her a gentle workout. Or else let her see the location on the beach where she'll be working tomorrow."

"Gotcha," Tom replied abruptly, glancing quickly at Nathan and Kami in the cab. "I sure wouldn't want to get in anyone's way."

Oh, no! Kami wanted to lean out and tell him, *It's not like that. Nathan's way out of my league, just like you and Coreen.* But she was too embarrassed to say anything.

Meanwhile, Nathan began to fill Kami in on some of the backdrop to the scenes being filmed this morning. "This is where Krystal, Coreen's character, is in a big fight with her dad, played by Matt. She's aiming to ride her horse on the beach when she should be in school. Mean Dad yells at her, says he's going to sell the horse to punish her."

Kami nodded. "I read that part."

"Cool. Krystal goes crazy – no way is Mean Dad going to sell her beloved horse. She runs to the stables and jumps in the saddle. Cue your out-of-control gallop along the beach, Kami."

By now, Jack had driven them slowly down a sandy lane towards a low, forested headland and a parking lot filled with trucks containing cameras and sound equipment.

"You OK?" Jack checked with Kami as he looked for a spot to park the trailer.

This is really happening! Kami thought as she picked out Brad and Matt surrounded by crew. She took a deep breath.

"Sure, she's OK," Nathan answered for her as he opened the door and jumped down from the cab. He gave Kami a big smile and offered his hand for her to follow. "Dude, it's not Kami we have to worry about – it's Coreen."

No sooner said than a silver SUV with shaded windows bumped along the track and came to a halt next to Magic's trailer.

"Here she is now," Nathan warned as the car door opened and the teen star of *Moonlight Dream* stepped out, head held high and long blonde hair flowing as she threw back her shoulders and launched into a catwalk, look-at-me strut. "Fasten your seat belts, guys. Enjoy the ride!"

"Action!"

Kami felt she could reach out and touch the tension in the air as Brad Morley's assistant director called for silence and the cameras rolled.

Matt stood beside the sand dunes that bordered the long strip of white beach. He eyeballed Coreen and yelled at her. Coreen yelled back – boy, was she good at yelling!

"Krystal, you don't have a choice – you have to stay in school and study!"

"Why do I? School sucks. I want to fetch Moonlight from the stable and you can't stop me!"

"Watch me," Mean Dad muttered, and the camera followed him as he strode towards a house overlooking the beach.

Coreen/Krystal chased after him. "What are you doing?"

"What's it look like I'm doing? I'm going into the house and I'm calling the dealer."

"The horse dealer?"

"Got it in one. Your precious Moonlight is going back to the sale barn, end of story," said Mean Dad, and he disappeared inside.

"Dad, wait!" Krystal began to run after him, then she stopped. She paused for a second before turning and running towards the stable block at the side of the house.

"Cut!" Brad Morley called. "Good work, everyone."

It was now time for Jack to pace out Magic and Kami's action sequence. He explained the back story as they walked.

"Krystal has defied her dad and ridden Moonlight along the shore, but he sticks with his plan to send the horse back to the sale barn. Early next morning he tries to load her horse into a trailer, but Krystal's there first and Moonlight is already tacked up. She fights with her dad, flings open the yard gate and tells Moonlight to run for his life."

"That's where me and Magic come in?" Kami asked.

"Magic gallops to the shoreline, then he stops and waits." Jack identified a spot on the beach marked by a small yellow flag.

"You hear that?" Kami asked Magic. "You gallop to the flag, then you wait for me."

Magic breathed out through relaxed lips.

"Then, Kami, you run from the yard towards Magic. Don't worry about where the cameras are. Your job is to focus on Magic and execute the stunt."

"Which side do I mount?"

"From the left," Jack told her. "Then, once you're in the saddle, rein Magic towards the ocean and launch into a lope."

"Lope." Kami repeated the instruction, internalizing every word Jack said.

"Pick up speed and gallop him into the water, through the breaking waves."

"Cool." Kami nodded and smiled at Magic. "You'll love that."

"After fifty metres from the flag, expect a guy walking his dog to suddenly appear. They'll come out of the forest and across the dunes. The dog will run at Magic and spook him."

"Spook," Kami echoed. "That's when Magic rears and tosses me out of the saddle?"

Jack nodded. "We need a saddle fall to the left followed by a left-foot drag."

"Got it." Now that she'd walked it through with Jack and knew exactly what she had to do, Kami was ready for her stunt-riding debut. "Let's do it," she told Magic, leading him back to the yellow flag.

"Action!" The director had his cameras in position. Magic had galloped across the white sand and stood at the water's edge while Kami waited in the stable yard.

She set off at a run, the wind blowing her hair from her face, salt from the ocean spray making her skin tingle. Her bare feet sank into the soft sand until she reached the water, where it was firmer and she managed to pick up speed.

Magic stood patiently. He didn't flinch when Kami reached him and leaped into the saddle.

"Good boy," she murmured, sitting deep and kicking him lightly. She felt the strength of his hindquarters as he rocked back, then launched himself into a strong lope.

Getting into his stride, Magic picked up speed and galloped through the shallow, white-crested waves, kicking up spray that sparkled in the sun. Ten metres, twenty metres galloping through the clear, shallow water, with endless turquoise ocean to their left, dunes and trees to their right. Thirty metres. Kami and Magic worked beautifully together. Forty metres, then fifty. The man and dog appeared right on cue. The dog had been trained to bark, then run at the horse, with the man helpless to stop him.

Magic and Kami saw the lean, black dog. Kami gave her horse the signal to spook and rear and within a split second Magic broke his stride, twisted away from the dog and raised himself on to his back legs. Kami was thrown off balance so fast and hard that she lost her reins.

"Good boy!" she whispered again, as Magic's front hooves landed close to the dog's head and the dog cringed and crept away, back to his master. Pressure from her left leg told Magic to wheel round to the right, again so hard and fast that it appeared that Kami had lost her balance. She fell to her left, clean out of the saddle, keeping her foot hooked into the stirrup so that when Magic launched himself into another gallop, she was dragged through the shallow waves.

Ten, fifteen – Kami counted Magic's strides. Thank goodness this was happening in water, she thought. Water and soft sand cut down on the bruises at least. On the count of twenty she kicked free.

"Cut!" Brad Morley yelled through his megaphone. "Terrific job, Kami. You're a natural!"

She was up on her feet, soaked through, feeling her

ribs ache a little as she took a deep breath. Magic slowed to a canter, then turned to come back to her. "Magic, you were more than terrific, you were totally perfect!" she sighed, throwing both arms round his neck.

Back at Five Sisters and already changed out of her wet dress, Kami set about giving Magic a full pampering session. She took off his saddle, then brushed the sand out of his mane and tail. Then she hosed him down to get rid of the salt from the sea water.

"Feels good, huh?" she asked.

Lowering his head, Magic shook himself all over, swishing his tail and showering Nathan and Tom who stood nearby.

"Sorry about that," Kami giggled.

"No, you're not," Nathan laughed.

"No, really," Kami shrieked as Nathan made a grab for the hose and aimed it right at her. Kami ducked out of the way.

"Oops." The jet of water hit Tom full in the chest. "Sorry, dude. Kami, what are you doing, putting your stunt-riding buddy into the firing line?"

"It's cool," Tom muttered, though his body language said different. He turned his back on Nathan and Kami, lifted Legend's saddle from the rail, then carried it off to the barn without saying another word.

Kami frowned. She felt bad for Tom.

Nathan handed the hosepipe back to Kami and she finished hosing down Magic's belly and legs.

"Where were you earlier?" Kami asked Tom when he came back. He was still dripping after his accidental soaking. "I didn't see you and Legend down at the beach."

Tom still refused to look at her as he shook his head. "We decided to ride through the forest instead."

"Dude, you missed Kami's debut," Nathan told him. "A new star was born."

"Magic was the star," Kami insisted as she turned off the hose. She walked him out to the meadow with Nathan still in tow. Looking over her shoulder, she noticed that Tom had walked off in the opposite direction.

"I mean it, Kami," Nathan insisted as she opened the gate and let Magic loose. "You're a great rider."

"Thanks, but I could never do what you and Coreen

do in front of a camera – no way!"

"You're kidding?"

"No. Learning a script, remembering my lines, acting it out and making it seem real – I couldn't do it. I mean, just look at the scene Coreen did this morning, the fight with her dad."

"She's a good actor," Nathan acknowledged, then hesitated. "The best. It's just..."

Kami closed the gate, then leaned against it, giving Nathan a searching look. "Is this something to do with the secret Coreen didn't want me to know?"

"There's a problem," Nathan admitted. "She'll probably shoot me down in flames for discussing this, but I – we need to do something."

"About what?" Kami was growing more and more curious.

"Let me ask you a question." Pacing to and fro, Nathan glanced towards the catering trailer where cast and crew had gathered for lunch. He spotted Coreen, sitting at a table with Matt and Jack. "Have you noticed how Coreen acts when she's around horses?"

"You mean, when she first came to Stardust?" Kami

thought back to Nathan and Coreen's visits to the stable yard.

"Yeah. I mean, do you remember when she refused to ride the horse?"

Still puzzled, Kami shrugged. "She was more interested in texting her friends, I guess."

Nathan nodded. "The texting stuff – that was a front. Just like the hair flicking and the head-in-the-air ignoring everyone."

"A front for what? What exactly is Coreen hiding?"

Nathan came to a halt right next to Kami and sighed. "You know how some people love horses and some people are terrified of them? Or do you just figure everyone loves them as much as you do?"

"No, I get it. Horses are hundreds of pounds of solid muscle and they're strong. Plus, their kick can do a lot of damage."

"So they're unpredictable and dangerous?"

"Only if you don't know what to look out for."

"But people who are scared of horses don't know what to look out for – that's my point. I tried to speak to Coreen afterwards and she was shaking like a leaf. Her hands were trembling so much she couldn't even press the right keys on her phone."

"At the idea of riding a horse?" Kami said in a disbelieving tone.

Nathan nodded. "Or of going anywhere near one, actually."

Kami frowned and took time to think this through. "Will she need to do that?" she asked.

"Yeah, after you leave," Nathan explained. "You know that there's a guy named Scott Maxwell in charge of the horses on this movie? His official title is head wrangler. Well, he's found three horses identical to Magic to double up as Moonlight in the scenes that don't involve any stunts. That's when Coreen has to get up close and personal with 'Moonlight' to shoot the non-stunt-riding scenes."

"I didn't know that," Kami admitted. But it made sense – there would be scenes between Krystal and Moonlight in the stable, with lots of close-up camera angles that only Coreen could do.

"It happens all the time. You guys get to do the exciting stunts, but you're only on set for a week at most, then you move on to work on something else and leave us to do the boring stuff!"

Just then, Nathan saw his co-star get up from the table and start to walk in their direction, so he speeded up the explanation. "It's got worse since our first visit to Stardust. Coreen's made up this story for Brad that she has an allergy, she gets asthma and comes out in a rash whenever she goes near a horse, blah-blah."

"So that she doesn't have to do any horse-related scenes?"

"Exactly. But no way will Brad buy that. The focus of *Moonlight Dream* is Krystal's relationship with her horse and how the character I play helps save the horse from the sale barn. If she spins the allergy story, Brad will turn round and tell her to take some antihistamines. She'll have to do the scenes anyway. Otherwise he'll fire her from the movie."

Kami glanced round. Coreen was heading their way, frowning and looking suspicious. "You're saying that we need to solve the problem for Coreen to stay in the role?"

"The bottom line is, can you make her love her horse?" Nathan wanted to know.

"How long have I got?" Kami asked.

"Until tomorrow morning, when Coreen shoots her

first scene with Moonlight." Putting on a fake, reassuring smile, he got ready to greet Coreen. "Can you do it?" he asked Kami out of the side of his mouth.

"I'll try," she decided, opening the gate to fetch Magic. "What do you say we start right now!"

chapter nine

"Nathan, I don't know how you could do this to me!" Coreen yelled. She stood with Nathan, Kami and Magic in the small meadow behind the trailers. "It was our secret!"

"I only told Kami because I reckon she can help," he protested.

"I don't need help!" she said.

"Listen, Coreen, either you let Kami teach you how to make friends with horses or you lose your job!" Nathan tried to reason with his co-star, but she was so angry that she didn't seem to care who else heard. "You have to learn not to be scared, that's all I'm saying."

"But you told ... *her*!" With a dismissive flick of her hand, Coreen let Kami know that she wasn't worth talking to directly. "Nathan, she's a no-name stunt double. They can hire any one of ten girls to step in and do her job, and you have to make sure she understands that."

"Whoa!" he objected. "Kami's cool, you can trust her."

"Nathan was only trying to help." Kami felt the sting of Coreen's insults, but she still stepped in to try and halt her meltdown. "And I'm not going to say anything. This is still a secret, believe me."

Coreen stepped back until she felt she was a safe distance from Kami and Magic. "Keep him right away from me," she begged. "Look at his eyes. Honestly, I can't even stand the way they stare at me!"

Kami held tight to Magic's lead rope. She shook her head and stayed quiet because whatever she said or did only seemed to make things worse.

"He's still staring!" Coreen cried, covering her face with her hands. "I think I'm going to faint!"

"This isn't going to work," Kami whispered to Nathan.

"And now you're both talking behind my back and making fun of me!" cried Coreen.

Still holding her hands in front of her eyes, she wheeled round and began to run. As she reached the gate she stumbled and almost collided with Jack, who'd come looking for Kami to check she was ready for the afternoon's filming.

"You can only help someone who wants to be helped," Jack declared when Kami clammed up over the disaster that had occurred. "No need to break any promises," he told her. "Coreen was yelling at the top of her voice so I heard every word."

"I guess." Kami sighed. They'd reached the yard where the trailer was parked, so she lowered the ramp for Jack to lead Magic in. "Coreen said something that really hurt," she confessed quietly, smoothing down her long blue dress, which Wanda had dried and pressed during lunch. "She said I wasn't special, that a whole load of girls could step in and do my job."

"Not true," Jack said firmly, loading Magic, then coming back down the ramp.

Kami smiled. "Thanks, Jack. But you're right, Coreen wasn't ready to listen to advice, especially not from me."

"Come on, get in the cab," he told her. "You tried to help; you did what you thought was right. Now you have to tell yourself it's not your problem."

Kami knew that what Jack said made sense, so she tried to focus on the scene scheduled for the afternoon. "This is where Magic gets to play the hero, right?"

"Yeah. I'll walk you through it when we get to the beach, but basically this scene follows on from the one we shot this morning. You fall to the ground and you lie unconscious. The tide comes in. Magic tries to revive you, but he can't make you open your eyes. When the waves lift you and carry you out to sea, he swims to the rescue."

"That is so cool!" said Kami.

"It's complicated to make Magic understand what we want him to do; I warned Brad that it won't be easy, especially with the time pressure we're under due to the tides. My idea is to swim alongside Magic in rehearsal, to show him. Then when we actually shoot the scene, I'll be able to stand on the sideline and yell instructions."

"Magic's very smart," Kami reminded Jack as he chose the same parking space as before and they jumped down from the cab. "He'll soon pick it up."

"You're happy with the floating out to sea part?" he

checked. "There'll be boats and lifeguards, plus the guy from the American Humane Association ready and waiting."

"I haven't swum in the ocean since I was a kid," Kami admitted. "But I'm a strong swimmer - I've been swimming in Clearwater Lake since I was four years old, so I'll be fine." She lowered the ramp and stepped inside the trailer. "Come on, Magic, let's get to work."

It was weird playing dead at the edge of the ocean and letting waves lap around you. Kami had to keep her eyes closed and allow her body to totally relax, trusting the lifeguards in a nearby boat to keep a look out and not let her come to any real harm.

"So, everyone knows what we're doing and we're ready for action," Brad had announced over the sound of waves crashing on to the shore. He'd checked that Jack was in place off camera with Magic, waiting for his cue. Then he'd asked Kami to take up position. Now here she was, lying at the water's edge as if she'd just fallen from her horse, feeling the cold, shallow water curl around her then lift her as wave after wave met the shore. Then she sensed herself being gently carried out to sea.

It happened fast. The water was surprisingly powerful, raising her up as Jack released Magic and let him splash towards her, calling instructions as he went. She heard the horse wade chest-deep through the breaking waves; felt him nudge her "lifeless" body with his nose, then tried not to react as another strong wave came in and the current sucked at her and bore her away.

Eyes closed! she reminded herself. *Trust Jack and Magic to get it right!* There would be a count of ten, then he would be with her again, swimming strongly, nudging and pushing, willing her to open her eyes.

Eight, nine, ten. Right on cue she felt Magic swim alongside her. Now she could open her eyes and react, she could raise an arm and drape it round his neck, then slowly, slowly clamber on to his back. Slump forward, don't look up. Let Magic swim for the shore.

The white waves crashed, the sun beat down from a clear blue sky. Magic swam until his feet hit the bottom and he waded out.

"Good boy," she breathed.

"Cut!" the director called.

Not a foot wrong; job done in a single, successful take.

Kami saw Brad give Jack a high five, and she caught sight of Tom behind them, wearing his Clearwater Tigers baseball cap. *Cool,* she thought. *I'm glad he came.* She smiled at him as he ran forward to take Magic from her while Wanda wrapped her in a beach robe and hurried her off the set.

"No way do I believe this is your first stunt-riding job." Nathan sat at supper with Kami, Jack and Tom.

"Kami only came to Stardust Stables at the start of the summer," Jack explained. "She's a fast learner, plus she bonded right away with her horse."

"Stop! I'm embarrassed," Kami pleaded. They'd been talking about her non-stop since they sat down to eat. "Let's change the topic."

"Tom, you're not saying much. Do you want to run through tomorrow's action sequence?" Jack suggested.

Tom shook his head. "I read the script. I already know what we have to do." Pushing his plate away, he stood up and muttered that he had stuff to be getting on with.

"Do we know what's wrong with him?" Jack asked Kami as Tom walked off. "He's not sick, is he?"

"I don't think so." Kami was about to follow him and find out what the problem was, but Nathan put his hand on her arm.

"What about you? Do you have stuff to do?" he asked quietly.

Surprised by his touch, she felt herself blush, then shook her head.

"So, sir, is it OK if I spend time with Kami?" Nathan asked Jack, super-polite.

Jack nodded. "But it's nine already and we're on early start tomorrow, so take care not to stay up too late," he warned. Then he followed Tom out of the dining room.

Nathan grinned at Kami. "Let's walk," he suggested, leading the way outside.

She followed, heart racing, into the warm, moonlit yard. The sweet scent of jasmine growing to either side of the ranch-house door filled the air and they strolled together down the driveway towards the dark forest beyond the gates.

"You're not scared by the dark?" Nathan checked, putting an arm round her shoulder. "Course not, what am I thinking? You're the girl who played dead and risked being carried out to sea."

"No, I'm not scared," she agreed, trying to match Nathan's long stride. This was unbelievable – she was walking with Nathan Atwood in the moonlight and he had his arm round her shoulder! *Breathe! Focus!* she told herself. "But I'll tell you what does scare me. Not 'what' but 'who', actually."

"Let me guess. We're talking Coreen?"

"Yeah."

"Sorry, she went a little crazy earlier."

"I guess it happens a lot?" By now they were deep in the forest, catching only glimpses of the silver moon through thick pine branches. Kami was surprised to see that her question had thrown Nathan off balance and made him take his arm away from her shoulder. "Sorry. Go ahead and tell me it's not my business."

"Don't be sorry. It's just that Coreen may look like a prima donna and I make jokes about her acting up to her star billing, but actually she isn't usually mean to people the way she was to you earlier today. She must be really screwed up about all this horse stuff. Seeing her reaction to Magic made me realize what she must be going through, and how we're running out of time."

"You two know each other well?"

"We came up through stage school together, and we've already been in two movies together as juvenile leads, playing brother and sister. *Moonlight Dream* is our third, the first where we have a romantic connection."

"You're really close," Kami decided, increasingly intrigued by the fact that Coreen Kessler, the girl who seemed to have it all, had problems the same as anyone else.

"Since Coreen first freaked out over riding the horse at your place, she's blown the whole thing out of proportion, turned it into some kind of phobia. When Brad finds out, she'll be in serious trouble," Nathan confided. "But, Kami, I still think you could help her."

"Only if she'll let me," she sighed, recalling Jack's advice. They fell silent in the thick darkness of the forest, then she spoke again. "Do you know where Coreen is now?"

"I saw her before dinner. She said she wasn't hungry and went straight to her room."

There was another long silence while Kami turned back and retraced her steps with Nathan at her side. "Go get her," she told him as they reached the iron gates at the entrance to Five Sisters. "Don't say anything, just bring her out to the meadow. No questions, just go!"

"You know people have problems," Kami told Magic when she found him tucking into alfalfa at the feeder in the meadow. "We humans make life more complicated than you equines."

Magic sighed, then went on munching hay.

"It's what we do. Take me and Nathan, for example. My heart went crazy for those ten seconds when he put his arm round my shoulder. Me and Nathan Atwood! But then I get it – he likes me, but only as a friend. I can tell that by the way he went on to talk about Coreen, kind of intense and serious. You can see he really, really cares about her!"

Magic munched some more.

"See, life's real easy for you. But take Coreen as another example. You saw how she was with you out here earlier – that girl has a total fear of horses."

Hearing something in the distance, Magic looked up and pricked his ears, his dark eyes glistening in the moonlight.

"What is it?" Kami strained her ears to hear. "Oh, it's Legend calling." She glanced round. The palomino was missing from the meadow, so Tom must have ridden her out under the stars. She turned back to Magic, stroking his ears. "Forget Legend and listen to me. Coreen has a problem and she's too proud to ask for help. But tomorrow's crunch day, she can't hide it any longer."

Magic tilted his head to one side in his usual way.

"Listen, I have a plan..."

Kami was still waiting for Coreen and Nathan when Tom and Legend returned. They stopped at the gates to the meadow, the palomino's pale mane and tail shining silver in the moonlight.

"Hey, where have you been?" Kami called.

"I wanted some alone-time, so we went down to the beach to watch the waves."

"Mesmerizing, huh?" Kami walked to the gate and opened it for them.

Tom nodded. "I could watch them forever."

This was the first time Kami had talked with Tom in what felt like ages, and she was glad to break down some of those awkward silences. "Magic heard Legend calling."

He nodded. "We loped through the shallow waves. Legend loved it. Then we headed back through the forest."

Kami smiled. "I wish I'd been there with Magic."

"Maybe next time," Tom said as he rode Legend towards the feeder at the far side of the meadow.

"Walk and talk," Nathan told Coreen, as he steered her towards the meadow at the far side of the ranch house. "Come on, Cori, share with me."

"What's to talk about?" she asked miserably.

"You, your brilliant career – everything."

"My so-called career is about to U-turn and you know it."

"Not necessarily," he argued.

"Yes, necessarily. You read our contracts – working with horses is part of the deal. I should have told my agent no way, right at the start."

"OK, but you didn't, and so here we are." Nathan stopped beside the make-up trailer and took both of Coreen's hands in his. "What do you want to do? Do you want me to go find Brad, tell him you're wimping out?"

"I am not wimping out!" Suddenly fiery, Coreen pulled her hands free.

"That's what everyone will say – 'Coreen Kessler in meltdown. Kessler can't take the pressure. Coreen's career on the rocks'."

She slowly let out a long, deep breath and then quickly inhaled, pulling back her shoulders. "OK, Mister Know-it-all, I'm not, I repeat, I am *not* wimping out!"

"So?" he grinned.

"So, I am rising to the challenge," she insisted, head up, shoulders back, taking more deep breaths.

"How?"

"By confronting my demons and beating my phobia."

"Like an arachnophobe learns to love spiders?"

"Exactly like that," Coreen insisted. "Find Kami. Get her to introduce me to the grey horse!" And she strode ahead of Nathan towards the meadow.

★★★★★

"Stand with me, here in the middle." Kami invited Coreen to stand with her in the bright moonlight. "Take this length of rope. I'll need you to snake the loose end through the dirt, like so."

Nervously Coreen took the rope and released one end experimentally along the ground.

"Good. OK, gather it up again. Now we walk up to Magic. We don't make eye contact - horses read that as an aggressive act." Kami crossed the meadow with Coreen until they stood roughly the rope's length away from Magic.

"This is way too close," Coreen complained, shaking from head to toe. "He's so big and scary. I have no clue what he's about to do."

"Look at Magic's ears," Kami told her. "They're pricked and pointed forward. That means he's alert, wondering what you're going to ask him to do. If his ears are flat against his head and his nostrils flare out, it tells you he's scared and getting ready to run. We don't want him to be scared. We want him to listen. So he's ready; release the rope again and snake it towards his back feet."

Coreen followed Kami's instruction and the sudden movement along the ground pushed Magic forward into a trot.

"Keep behind him, keep him trotting."

Coreen snaked the rope again, surprised that the horse understood the long-distance command.

"Use the rope, trot him until he starts to lower his head."

"I don't touch him with the rope?" Coreen asked.

"No, and don't look at his eyes. Keep him trotting."

Coreen nodded and kept on working with Magic, with Kami walking alongside.

After ten minutes, Kami spoke again. "OK, now Magic's head is going down – he's tired. Ease off with the rope, let him slow to a walk. Good. Now half turn away from him. Look, he's walking on, sticking close to the fence, but he's turning towards you and wondering what you want him to do next. You're going to ease up completely and let him get near you."

"Get near me?" Coreen echoed, as if this was still her worst nightmare.

"It's OK, you've kept him trotting and worked him

hard. He recognizes you're the boss, like the alpha male in any big herd. Now all he wants is to come close and be your friend."

"My friend?" Coreen sighed, still unsure.

"Yeah, you're in control, remember. No eye contact, just turn away a little more. Look, now he feels safe to approach you. His head's down. You're still the boss."

"Don't be scared, Cori." Nathan stood by the gate, his eyes glued on Coreen. "You can do it." He spoke under his breath so as not to wreck her concentration.

"Magic is stepping into your space. He's saying 'please let me in'." Kami smiled at Coreen. She'd used this technique a hundred times with new colts back home at Elk Creek. "So raise your hand slowly, eyes down, still don't look at him. Stroke him, say hi."

Slowly, one inch at a time, Coreen raised her hand to stroke Magic's neck. "So soft, so warm, so smart," she murmured, her voice full of wonder. "And so gentle."

"That's horses for you," Kami said softly. Then she grinned and stroked Magic's neck. They'd done it; Coreen had taken a first step on the road to conquering her horse phobia once and for all. *Thank you, Magic. Thank you for being you.*

chapter ten

"So, guys, we have a tight schedule," Brad Morley announced early next morning as he gathered crew and actors on the beach.

Jack, Kami and Tom had unloaded Legend and Magic from the trailer in time to hear the director's team talk.

"First, we shoot scene forty-three with Coreen and Nathan, plus the two horses." Glancing around, Brad noted the absence of Coreen as usual. "Where is she? Will someone tell her to get her butt down here now!"

As an assistant drove back to Five Sisters to hurry her along, Brad continued to give instructions. "Forty-three is where Moonlight carries Krystal back to the house – she's half drowned, remember. So, Nathan, you ride the palomino through the dunes and see she's in trouble.

You catch up with her and warn her that you heard her dad tell the horse dealer to come back later. The scene ends with Matt stepping off the porch, looking mean as hell."

"Now all we need is Coreen," Jack muttered. The horses were ready and everyone was in place except for her. "Tom, you can hand Legend over to Nathan for this scene. Check her cinch first. Kami, be ready to hand Magic over to Coreen."

Kami waited anxiously. Coreen's no-show surprised her and now she wasn't so sure how much last night's lesson had helped after all. One glance at Nathan's worried face told her that he feared the same thing. But then she relaxed – a silver SUV had arrived at the parking lot and Coreen stepped out, looking tense.

After that, everything happened fast. Brad checked camera angles one final time, Tom gave Nathan a leg up into the saddle, Wanda sprayed water over Coreen's blue dress to replicate the near-drowning episode and finally Coreen approached Kami and Magic.

"Coreen, we're all set up," Brad told her. "The light's perfect. Come on, let's shoot!"

"Ready?" Kami prompted, offering to help her into the saddle.

For a moment, Coreen hesitated. There was a big difference between bonding with Magic in a quiet, moonlit meadow and actually climbing up on the horse in the bright light of day in front of all these people. She turned to Nathan for support and saw him nod calmly and urge her on. "I'm ready," she decided.

Good work! Kami thought as she eased Coreen on to Magic's back. "Lean forward," she instructed. "Put both arms round Magic's neck and let him carry you slowly towards the house. Remember – trust him!"

"I can't believe I'm doing this!" Coreen groaned as she felt Magic shift his weight beneath her. But she did what Kami had told her as they waited for the cameras to roll.

"Go, girl!" Kami breathed as she stepped away. "Magic will look out for you. Nothing bad will happen."

Scene forty-three, Take one – Action! Magic carried Coreen up the beach. The camera caught her beautiful face in close-up, eyes closed, head resting against the horse's dark mane. It stayed on her as Nathan caught up with her before she reached the house. She heard him call her name and opened her eyes, raising her head from Magic's neck.

Cut! Take two. Rearrange Coreen's wet hair so that stray strands streak across her cheek. Tone down the mascara, enhance the paleness of her cheeks. Spray more water on the dress. Action!

Cut! Take three, Take four... Brad wanted the scene to be perfect. He altered camera angles to include more of Magic's face. He asked Coreen to slump further to one side as though she were in danger of falling off. Take five...

"I'm amazed," Jack admitted to Kami and Tom as they watched off camera. "No way does that girl look like she has a problem with horses."

"She doesn't, not any more," Kami answered with a satisfied smile. *Crisis totally over. Coreen's glittering career back on course.*

"Good, I got what I need," Brad decided at last. "Coreen, Nathan, take a break while we set up for the reverse shots. And thanks, guys, you both did a great job."

Brad Morley worked the Stardust team hard during their remaining days on location at Five Sisters.

On Wednesday afternoon he jumped ahead to scene seventy-eight and shot a sequence where Kami and Tom loped through the forest. This was the part in the *Moonlight Dream* plot after Coreen and Nathan's characters had decided to snatch Moonlight from his stable before the trailer could return to take him away to the sale barn. Kami, doubling up for Coreen, had to ride Magic bareback and in just a rope halter. The head wrangler Scott checked that Kami was OK with this, then gave her the go-ahead and watched her swerve between trees and duck under low branches on their flight from Mean Dad and the horse dealer.

Thursday morning was scene eighty-one – another forest scene where the runaways rode deeper into the forest and came across a logging operation at work. Tom and Kami had to ride Legend and Magic past sawing machinery and through an area where giant trees had been felled, picking their way over trunks until a tree crashed down close to where they rode and their horses spooked.

"Legend and Magic are in a blind panic," Jack

reminded them before the call for action. "They're out of control, jumping those high log piles to your left. The camera follows you as you jump. Tom, you get to the third pile, then Legend hits the logs, and you fall. Kami, you get Magic over the logs but you turn and go back for Tom."

It was a tricky stunt, especially since Kami rode without saddle or bridle and the territory was risky. No horse liked jumping over high, solid logs and loping through undergrowth. She hoped they could do it in one take.

"Let's get through this safely," she murmured to Magic as they waited for the director's call. "Then we can go back to the ranch and chill."

Magic snickered as if to say, *Stick with me.*

Next to her, Tom waited nervously with Legend.

She smiled at him, glad when he smiled back. "Cool hat," she grinned, thinking how good he looked in the beaten-up, dusty Stetson from Wanda's shelves. Then she settled her own straw hat more firmly on her head and turned up the collar of her checked shirt just the way Wanda had told her to.

"Likewise," he muttered.

Tom still wasn't talking much, even after their late-night conversation in the meadow, and this made her sad. Then again, maybe he was always like this on location, just serious and focused.

What happened to the old jokey Tom? she'd wanted to ask, pretty much ever since they arrived at Five Sisters. But Tom's barriers were up and it looked as if she'd have to wait until they got back to Stardust before she found out the answer. *I'll ask Kellie,* she thought. *His sister will know how to make him lighten up.*

The thought had hardly registered before Brad Morley gave the two young stunt riders the go-ahead. Tom and Kami set off side by side, ambling between trees at a relaxed trot until the signal came for them to make their horses rear and run. There was no actual logging machinery on set, and no scary chainsaws, so the two riders had to fake a reaction and set their horses into spook mode.

"Let's go, Magic!" Kami hissed as he rose on to his hind legs, plunged down, then set off at a crazy lope through the thick undergrowth. Their every move was captured from above by a camera mounted on a crane.

Tom and Legend kept pace, both horses clearing the

first and second log piles with ease.

"So far, so good!" Kami murmured. Magic's lope was smooth and safe. He soared high over the logs and landed evenly, forging on towards the next.

But the third pile was where Tom and Legend faked the fall. Kami felt them next to her, caught their blurred shape out of the corner of her eye, saw the obstacle loom up ahead.

Wham! Horse and rider were down and rolling on the ground in a controlled fall. She wheeled Magic round in time to see Legend go belly up with her legs in the air and Tom lying motionless.

"Cut!" Brad called.

Kami and Magic trotted back to the scene of the "accident". "OK, Tom, you heard what he said. You can get up now."

Legend rolled, folded her legs under her and stood up. Tom lay still.

"Tom!" Quickly Kami slid to the ground and bent over him. "Tom, get up!"

For a moment everything stopped.

Then Tom opened one eye. "Gotcha!" he grinned as he leaped to his feet.

★★★★★

"That was so not funny!" Kami was still not over the fright Tom had given her earlier, as they walked Magic and Legend out to the meadow at the end of the day. "All week you've been acting like the sulky kid at the back of the class and now suddenly you're the joker again."

He laughed as they took off the horses' head collars and watched them make straight for the fresh alfalfa. "You should've seen the look on your face!"

"Seriously, I thought my heart was going to jump clean through my ribs," Kami complained, closing the gate after them. "I don't know what's got into you lately – moody one minute, playing tricks on me the next."

"Nothing's got into me," he said with a shrug.

"Yes, it has. You're different."

"No, I'm not."

"You didn't even come to see me shoot my very first scene on the beach," she reminded him.

Tom gave another shrug. "I didn't think you'd noticed."

"What? Why not?" said Kami.

Tom shrugged and looked a bit embarrassed.

"Well, I did. And I also noticed that you've practically stopped speaking to me since then."

"I told you, I've had things to do."

"And now you play dead and scare the life out of me! What was *that* all about?"

"I don't know. I guess I couldn't resist."

Kami sighed. *Jeez, this is like squeezing blood from a stone.* She was almost glad to hear footsteps and see Coreen hurrying to join them.

Tom saw her, too. "Catch you later," he told Kami and quickly slipped away.

"I hope you're giving your horse plenty to eat," Coreen began cheerily. She took her phone from her jeans pocket and used the camera to snap Magic tucking into supper. "So cute!" she beamed. "I'm going to put the pictures on my Facebook page, show the whole world how beautiful he is."

Kami smiled back. "How many friends do you have on Facebook?"

"Over a million."

"You hear that, Magic – a million! You're going to be famous!"

"And I'll tell everyone you're a terrific rider," Coreen

promised. "I'll even come clean and tell them I was terrified of horses until you came along and cured me."

"You don't have to do that," Kami told her, looking embarrassed. "I'm just happy it worked out."

Putting away her phone, Coreen's face grew serious. "No, really, I want to say sorry for being a total nightmare. Can you forget the nasty stuff I dumped on you?"

"You were under pressure," Kami said.

"Yeah. I didn't mean what I said."

"That's OK. I understand."

"And I want to say thank you, Kami."

"Thank Nathan, too. It was his idea," Kami reminded her.

Coreen nodded. "Nathan knows me better than anyone. We grew up together."

"He told me. You know he really cares about you?"

"I do." Coreen's smile was wistful at first, then her mouth twitched and turned mischievous. "So, Kami, how about you and Tom?"

"Tom?" Kami blushed, surprised that it had been so obvious. "Not the same," she insisted. "We didn't meet until I joined the stunt-riding team. Tom doesn't know me well at all."

"No?" Coreen refused to step aside as Kami tried to get past.

"No. You've seen him lately, he hardly even speaks to me."

"But he looks at you plenty. When you're working out stunts with Jack, Tom watches you like a hawk. And when he sees you talking with Nathan, he turns round and walks the other way."

"He does?" Kami coloured up even more.

"He walks away because he's jealous," Coreen insisted.

"No, he can't be!" Flustered, Kami refused to believe what she was being told.

Coreen's smile broadened. "Let me spell it out slowly," she said. "In words of one syllable so that you get it. Kami: Tom – likes – you, period."

Kami was shell-shocked. Could what first Kellie and now Coreen had told her actually be true? And was that why jokey Tom had turned into Moody Boy all of a sudden? She had to find out, but it took all her courage to go looking for him later that evening.

"Ask me to do a saddle fall, Roman riding, a back vault, a drag, a front wing – I don't care how many bruises I get. I'd do anything rather than this," she muttered to Magic as she checked the meadow. "What if it turns out that Kellie and Coreen have got it wrong? What if he cuts me dead? How stupid will I feel!"

Magic listened, then did his speciality head-tilt thing.

"But I have to talk to him," she decided, turning from the gate and spotting Tom in the entrance to the barn. She swallowed hard and walked over.

Tom didn't react as she approached, just leaned against the doorpost, hat pulled down over his forehead and arms folded.

"So," she began. "Tomorrow we pack up and fly home. We let Scott Maxwell's other stand-ins take over from here."

Tom raised an eyebrow.

"I can't wait to see Kellie and the girls again. And Becca. I texted her and she says Pepper's leg is healing OK." Whoa, this was hard work. She still wasn't getting a reaction, so she chirped more nonsense about phoning home to find out how Columbine was getting along without her and if Squeaky had had her kittens yet. "Sorry, I'm an idiot," she ended breathlessly. "I don't usually ramble on and on..."

"Yeah, don't waste your breath on me," Tom mumbled, turning away and checking Legend's tack hanging on a nearby hook. "Go find Nathan and say your goodbyes, exchange phone numbers, leave him your email address, whatever."

"Nathan?" It was true, Tom was jealous! "You don't think he... I don't... We aren't..."

"Come on, Kami, spit it out."

"Nathan and I are not an item," she gabbled. "That's stupid."

"Well, thanks for calling me stupid," he grunted.

"No, that's not what I meant at all." Talk about digging a deeper hole – this one was big enough to bury herself in. So she took a long breath and tried to explain more calmly. "Sure, I had a crush on him, just like you did with Coreen. Who could help it?"

"I watched you. It looked like more than a schoolgirl crush," Tom muttered.

"Yeah, well, if you'd been around more, you'd know that Nathan doesn't act like a big movie star – in fact, he's an all-round nice guy. He knew this was my first stunt-riding job so he showed me the ropes, helped me settle in, that's all."

Tom cleared his throat and tried to sound calm and collected. "It's cool, Kami, I was out of line with the Nathan comment. Forget I said anything."

"What I'm saying is– Oh God, I don't know what I'm saying!" She was done; she didn't know how to make things better. She backed out of the barn, shaking her head.

"Kami." Tom let her get halfway across the yard before he spoke.

She turned.

He came right up to her and slowly leaned in, locking eyes with her. "You want to ride along the beach with me one last time?" he asked.

Legend and Magic matched each other stride for stride. They loped along the water's edge as the sun sank over the flat, sparkling horizon.

Kami sat deep in the saddle, hair blowing free, hearing the splash of the horses' hooves and the call of gulls overhead. She glanced at Tom, whose Stetson was still low on his forehead, and he smiled back at her.

"Race you to the rocks," he suggested.

"You hear that, Magic?" Kami murmured, loosening her reins and letting him run free.

Her horse exploded out of a lope into a gallop and surged forward, kicking up spray. Beside them, neck and neck, Tom crouched low in the saddle like a race-horse jockey. The dappled grey versus the palomino, silhouetted against the red setting sun, only slowing to a halt as they ran out of white sand and came to the rocky, forested headland.

"Dead heat?" Kami asked, leaning forward to pat Magic's neck.

Tom grinned and nodded. "Not a hair's breadth between us."

Together they turned their horses and started the long walk back along the sand.

chapter eleven

"Kami and Magic did an OK job," Jack reported to Lizzie.

It was late Friday afternoon, and everyone was hanging out at Stardust Stables, listening to Jack's feedback. The horses were fed and watered and taking a well-earned rest after their long trip home.

"Only 'OK'?" Kami whispered to Alisa. "Not even 'good'?"

"Don't stress – he's keeping down the praise because he doesn't want your head to grow too big for your hat," Alisa whispered. "We can't afford a new one!"

Kellie agreed. "'OK' from Jack is the most anyone ever gets around here."

Lizzie smiled at Kami, then came up and gave her a quick hug. "I knew you could do it," she murmured.

Kami grinned back. Boy, was she glad she and Magic were home and in one piece.

"A star in the making!" Hayley grinned.

"So, how was Nathan Atwood in the flesh?" Kellie chipped in.

The girls had run to meet Kami off the trailer, desperate for an update. They'd all taken care of the two horses, then crowded round her, begging for details of the *Moonlight Dream* shoot, ignoring Tom, who was, of course, an old hand at stunt riding.

"Yeah, Kami, is Nathan as much of a hunk as he is in his movies?"

"Totally. Anyway, you saw him here on the yard – swoon factor ten out of ten."

"No hidden flaws?" Alisa pressed.

"Not one. The opposite, actually."

"Oh, poor Tom," Kellie sighed, turning to him. "Nathan perfect this, Nathan screen god that. How can a humble stunt rider compete?"

"Not possible," he agreed, avoiding looking at Kami.

"Quit teasing your brother," Hayley told Kellie.

"Actually, it's no contest," Kami told the girls. And, smiling, she stole a quick glance at Tom.

"So Pepper's leg is healing," Becca told Kami.

It was Friday evening and they were in the row of stalls where Kami had first set eyes on Magic. Pepper stuck his head over the partition, looking for sympathy, which the two girls gave him in spades.

"The vet says no more painkillers, but still to rest it for a week. After that, we're back in action, aren't we, Pepi?"

Kami rubbed Pepper's nose. "Great news. And what about Pete Mason?"

"Sshh! Don't even say that name around here."

"Didn't the cops do anything?"

"The sheriff went to his place to 'talk' with him. Mason swore he was nowhere near Stardust Stables when our horses broke loose and he has an alibi, so it's Tom's and your word against his. Which means he's still out there, free to carry on with his campaign to sabotage Stardust."

"Not good," Kami sighed.

"The sheriff did warn him, though. He said they would be keeping a close eye on him for the next few weeks."

"Better."

"Lizzie was in shock at first – even she didn't think her ex would play that dirty. But now she just shrugs and says don't look back," Becca reported. "She's a 'glass-half-full' person. Anyway, we did get new business contracts while you were away."

"Hey, you two!" Hayley walked by with a bucket of grain for Cool Kid, who was stabled two stalls further down the row, greedily looking out for his extra feed. "Kellie said for you to join her, Ross and Alisa by the cold drinks machine. They want to party."

So Kami and Becca gave Pepper a final pat, then crossed the yard in the last of the day's sunshine.

"So what new contracts do we have?" Kami asked Kellie as she and Becca joined the small group sitting round the table under the yellow umbrella.

"Dylan and I got the cattle-rustling TV series, remember." Kellie's broad smile almost split her face in two. "We trailer Dylan out to Texas later this summer."

"And Diabolo and I auditioned and got a 'maybe' for the *Wildfire* movie," Alisa reported. "We should hear for sure after the weekend."

Kami nodded happily, then silently wondered where

her next job would take her and Magic - California again, New Mexico, Canada... Whatever it was, wherever they went, they sure would work hard here in the round pen to improve their vault tricks and shoulder stands, their front wings and one-foot drags. "It's going to be a great summer," she said.

With a great team, she added to herself as the group split off to do laundry, sweep the tack room and scoop poop before supper.

She waved at Tom and Zak riding the tractor, taking alfalfa out to the meadow, then she crossed the yard and climbed the gate after them. Magic spotted her and loped to meet her.

"Happy to be home?" Kami asked, sitting astride the gate and reaching out to stroke him.

He ducked his head and snorted.

"Me, too," Kami sighed, not wanting to change a thing as she watched the sun slip down behind the mountains and the valley slowly fall silent. "I'm totally happy with my life, right here, right now."

Look out for the next
Stardust Stables adventure –
coming soon!

SABLE HAMILTON
stardust
stables
WILDFIRE